THE DEER YARD

AND OTHER STORIES

TOM MAHONEY

Edited by JOE MAHONEY

Foreword by SUSAN RODGERS

Cover Illustration by ERIN MAHONEY

Cover Design by VALERIE BELLAMY

For Joseph Thomas
Mahoney
1900 - 1954

Writers turn dreams into print.

— JAMES A. MICHENER

CONTENTS

FOREWARD

SUSAN RODGERS

November 5, 2021

When I was six years old, my father took me with him to visit his family in Johnville, New Brunswick. My three siblings—Joe, Shawna, and Kathy—stayed at home in Summerside, Prince Edward Island, with Mom. While Dad and I were away, the workers on the ferries that traversed the Northumberland Strait between New Brunswick and Prince Edward Island went on strike, and Dad and I couldn't get home. In the early seventies, the

Confederation Bridge spanning the Northumberland Strait was a distant dream. Lucky me! I was given the gift of extra time with my father.

We stayed at his mother's home, a small white clapboard house trimmed with a deep, dark Irish green. One grey morning I watched my grandmother and her sister fervently pray the Rosary on their knees in a tiny bedroom. Spellbound, I watched from the tiny kitchen yonder. The quiet rhythm of their voices, thick stockings covering their legs even in the summer heat, full aprons over their cotton farm dresses—I knew not to speak, because I understood that I was being presented a glimpse into another world, another time. My eyes were stinging from the onions my grandmother had put in the pickles that she was boiling on the stove. Stirring that mass of swirling pickles as the women prayed, my small hands clasped around a big wooden spoon so I could summon up enough power to stir, I listened, and wondered what, or whom, they were praying for. My dad was away for the day, visiting his brother Ambrose at the old farmhouse up on the hill where, for so much of their youth, they had cared for animals, mended fences, and farmed potatoes. I was mystified, curious about this country cabin and the lives that flourished between its walls.

I wanted to know more.

In the evenings, my dad's brothers and sisters came around to chat. Tales were tall, laughter reigned, and sometimes the voices got hushed. There was an upright piano in the corner that vibrated whenever someone sat down to play it; next to it, a screen door that slammed hard when you let it go. Outside, empty barns, their livestock long gone, beckoned my imagination into earlier times. But this wasn't the farm where my father grew up. A thin ribbon of road that crested a hill once you passed the church, and then disappeared into thick woodlands somewhere far beyond, led to that cozy homestead a few miles away, hugged by thick woods. My imagination caught fire. What was life like for my father as a child, and as a curious teen, in this rural landscape? His father had passed away long before I was born. I couldn't help but wonder about my dad, and the grandfather I'd never known, living here where the breezes blew over the hilly land with unrestrained glee, and where praying the Rosary on one's knees was part of everyday life.

Back home later that summer, we dove back into our busy lives in our small island town. Johnville and its people faded into history. I was nine when my grandmother passed away. She was the first person I knew who died. With her went our trips to Johnville, and thus, to my dad's past.

It wasn't until many years later that Dad's short stories started coming. What a blessing! I soaked them up, amazed at my father's ability to fill in, with prose, so many of the blanks about his past, about his side of the family. Dad's tales bring to life his childhood on the farm. Many stories focus on his early teens and twenties. A few more modern stories give us a glimpse into his perspective on the world now. In this book, Dad's father comes back to life; his mother, brothers, and sisters leap off the pages. The animals Dad cherished in the thirties and forties are here too—cows and Clydesdales, and Toby the yellow farm dog. Toby was especially cherished—he appears in more than one story. My favourite story about Toby was once featured on Stuart McLean's beloved CBC radio show, The Vinyl Café. Toby is famous!

Dad's stories brim over with life. Poignant and heartwarming, and often laugh-out-loud funny, one story even musters up a century-old murder. The casual dialogue makes readers feel like they are right in the stories with the characters. Bears appear in sometimes startling ways, but always just doing what bears do. Nature is a character— rural farmland, rivers, hills dotted with wooden barns. Black flies buzz through the pages too, in the raspberry bushes on a hot summer day, and on a thin trail snaking its way through the woods by a riverbank.

A treasured letter from one of Dad's brothers is included in this compilation, an actual letter from his brother Bill as a young man. Its off-the-cuff language reveals down-home kinship and a pragmatic, yet humorous, peek at farm life.

My father is a natural storyteller. His stories are vivid. He writes with the five senses—his use of sound puts readers right in the setting. Often Dad tells a story within a story. You'll feel like you're there, sitting alongside the person to whom the tale is being told. The stories left me wishing that I was there amongst that family in those long-ago days, surrounded by a big, open sky and a beckoning, mysterious forest. I want to sit by a warm fire when the day's work is done, with fresh hot biscuits in my belly and a mug of tea cupped in my hands. It may have been lonely at times on that isolated farm back in the woods, and I know the days were long and the work hard, but life in the country before cellphones and computers sounds downright idyllic to me.

Dad's eighty-seven now. I always thought of him as a quiet man, but I see deeper now; I see the kind, observant soul that lived within many of these tales. I see the cozy country farmhouse with the busy family, all doing the best they could, I see the dusty wood box beside the stove and the much-loved yellow dog dozing peacefully next to it. I see the hilly potato field that was harvested with hands in the earth, not with machines, and I see horses drawing wagons, and salmon, plentiful, in the river.

Most of all, I see the man who took

the time to put these stories down on paper. I see, through his thoughtful eye and pen, just how much the world has changed over the last eighty-seven years and how much that change boggles his mind.

With his writing, Dad has reminded me that once there was a simpler time when people lived in the land and not on it, and where the best kind of lunch was a couple dozen crispy trout freshly hoisted from a river, and roasted over an outdoor fire.

Thank you, Dad.

- Susan

1

THE DEER YARD

The small farmhouse shook from the heavy onslaught of wind and snow. With an eerie whine and moan the wind whiffled around the eaves searching for entry. Tenuous drifts crept across the kitchen floor as fine dry snow sifted under the door. Outside, the swirling snow collected into huge drifts that buried roads and fences, anything in its path, as the relentless wind drove it onward. The two boys scratched tiny holes in the thick frost of the kitchen window so they could watch the winter storm roar past the open porch.

In the afternoon, with no change in the raging storm, the boys put on heavy coats and boots, thick mitts and scarves, and struggled toward the barn. The nervous animals were quiet, fearful of the howling wind and creaking beams, afraid the wooden structure might collapse on their heads. Timothy, the younger of the two at thirteen, cleaned the manure away from the milk cows, spread clean straw for bedding, and then forked in fresh hay for their dinner. As he buttoned his warm coat, pulling the collar close to his ears, he wondered how the forest animals fared in weather like this. When John, two years older, finished caring for the horses, the two brothers plunged through the drifts together, scrambling back to the house.

The storm blew itself out during the night. In the morning, the March sun rose to a fresh landscape of white and clean snow. Flocks of birds were soon about, famished from a day's abstinence. Rabbits began to stir, beating down fresh trails. Soon a young skier glided along over the snow, exploring the new world, curious about every track, every recent sign of life.

Timothy's heavy wooden skis slid smoothly forward, never mind the loose bindings and gum rubber boots providing minimum control.

He followed along a quiet country lane, blocked for the winter with snow. In summer it was a narrow dirt road where tree branches met overhead and squirrels and chipmunks scampered around. A thick hardwood growth covered the steep slope above the road. Below, glimpses of a split cedar fence could be seen. Timothy skied easily along until he came to the top of a low knoll, where he discovered that a huge drift had spread clear across the road, far enough to completely inundate the shrubs and rail fence below. He climbed onto the drift and followed it toward the edge where he found a lofty precipice, towering over an old pasture field.

Timothy braced the ski poles firmly in the snow, allowing the tips to extend beyond the edge of the drift. He peered nervously downward, thrilled by the wintry scene below. The steep sidehill field was strewn with young pine and yellow spruce. The morning sun sent long shadows out from every tree, almost hiding the long drifts created by the storm.

The young skier chose his path with care, steeled his nerves, and pushed forward with his poles to slide over the edge. He bent his knees to aid his balance as he plummeted downward, aiming for the drift to the right of the nearest tree. The cheap wooden skis were difficult to control, nearly throwing the inexperienced skier headfirst into the drift as they rode up and over. Timothy plunged downward again passing one tree on the left and another on the right as he weaved his way dangerously onward.

With snow flying, eyes watering and

heart pounding, Timothy gritted his teeth and hung on. When the hill levelled out, the young skier, excited and breathless, swung sideways and stopped. Shading his eyes from the sun, he looked back to see high above the drift he'd started from minutes before.

Starting back up the hill to try the run over again, he discovered deer tracks, deep impressions in the heavy snow leading upward along the trail his skis had just made.

"Where did you come from?" the boy wondered.

He leaned on his poles and surveyed the wasteland of snow. It didn't take long to figure out what must have happened. A small depression in a drift disclosed that the deer had sheltered from the storm tucked behind a tree. Overnight it had been completely buried by the drifting snow. Startled by Timothy's two wooden skis passing directly over its head, the frightened animal had emerged from its cocoon of snow and bounded away behind Timothy's back in the opposite direction.

The climb back up the hill went slower than Timothy expected. The new snow, soft and powdery, made for hard going. When he finally reached the top he discovered the big, wide imprints of snowshoe tracks on the old summer lane. It was difficult to suppress his excitement. The winter had been long and lonely. These tracks could mean company.

He crossed the road, climbed the bank to a field, and coasted down a long hill to the farmhouse. *That's Bob for sure,* he thought happily, observing the snowshoes alongside a pair of shoes on the porch. He loosened the straps, kicked the skis free, brushed away the loose snow, and stood the skis proudly next to the snowshoes.

Bob Tucker was a colourful character who lived in a small cabin out back of Carrol Mountain. When the days began to lengthen and the sun took on new warmth, Bob would leave his wife, kids, and cabin to visit old friends. He loved to fill up on hearty farm food, retell old stories, and play cards. Timothy's family was often his first stop. They had a battery radio, and Joe, Timothy's dad, would review all the war news, priming Bob for his next call, a visit to another lucky neighbour.

Timothy smelled tobacco smoke when he opened the door. Bob sat near the wood-box, close to the kitchen stove. He'd removed his heavy coat, but small puddles had formed beneath the soft leather moccasins still laced to his feet. Bob was a powerful man with strong arms and thick shoulders. There was a tinge of grey in his long hair and dirty beard. His attention seemed divided between the dinner preparations around him and his old friend Joe, who sat on the leather sofa across from him.

"Look what the storm blew in," Timothy said. "Why, hello Bob, how do the shoes work?"

Bob raised his pipe in greeting. "Just great. Much better than those sticks of yours. I saw where you went off that drift. You could've broken your neck."

"Oh, that was fun. No thrill in snowshoes. And I skied right over a big deer! It was buried in a drift."

"Sure you did," John chuckled, from where he slouched on top of the wood box.

Neither of the older men seemed surprised when Timothy described the deer tracks and the depression in the snow.

"Bob did that once on his snowshoes," Joe said.

Bob just lowered his head.

"Sit in," someone called.

Dinner at noon was the main meal on a farm. Money was scarce, while beef, potatoes, carrots and turnips were not. After making short work of his first helping, Bob looked anxiously around. Someone asked if perhaps he'd care for some more. He completed a second helping of meat and vegetables, topped off with fresh rolls.

Bob helped Joe hitch the team to a front bobsled and spent the afternoon breaking trails to keep the winter roads open. The boys had chores to do. They cleaned the stables, watered and fed the cows, cared for the pigs, and by the time the wood had been chopped and lugged into the house it was just about supper time.

Soon they were seated before a table loaded with liver, onions, fried potatoes, fresh biscuits, and apple pie—the girls had obviously been doing chores too. Bob had seconds all around except for the pie. Excitement began to build as the meal came to an end. A new story was coming, followed by a card game of Auction.

The girls cleared the table and washed the dishes as the men gathered around the sofa and poked fresh wood into the stove.

"How could anyone snowshoe over a

deer?" Timothy finally had a chance to ask.

"You were with me, Joe," Bob said, reloading his pipe. "Didn't you ever tell the boys about that trip we took?"

Joe said nothing, only shook his head, perhaps wondering whether this was one for the kids.

Bob had no such qualms. "You remember all the deer we saw that fall, Joe? We shot that big buck, and your mother bottled it. We had big jugs full of meat. Anyway, you were wondering where all the deer spent the winter and I figured they had to yard up at the old Ryan place. That's where we always saw them first in the spring. Soon as the fields started to bare, those deer came out in bunches. One day in April I saw over fifty, just finding their first feed of grass."

The Ryan place was part of an old settlement away back on the creek. The Ryans hadn't been able to make a living, so they'd just packed up and left, abandoning the place. The fields grew up into white spruce and alders. The houses rotted into the cellars. Some of the better fields were kept seeded in hay.

"We talked about those deer all fall, didn't we, Joe? You thought as how they yarded at the old mill dam. That place really grew into a thicket after the Ryans left it."

Joe remembered it all right. He was soon contributing to Bob's narrative. "I always wanted to see a deer yard, and there was only one way to do it. We left here one morning about daylight, middle of February, wasn't it, Bob? Never made it the first time, though. We gave it a good try. Still, I thought Bob would never go back again."

Bob frowned. "Don't bother with that now. Made it next time, didn't we? There was some bunch of deer in there, and they let us go right up to them."

The audience could sense the glow and animation in the two old friends as they recounted their adventure. Timothy wanted to know how old they were at the time but didn't dare interrupt to ask.

Bob continued. "We snowshoed back over the ridge, then straight on through the woods until we came to the creek. The snow on the ice made great going so we tramped right up the creek until we reached the dam, and there were the deer."

Joe carried on not missing a beat. "Lots of mud must have filled the old dam before it rotted out, so it grew up in heavy grass. The snow was a good ten feet deep in that hollow and the deer had beaten down all these narrow trails to get at the grass. We walked to the edge of the cuttings, not sinking a bit on our snowshoes, and we could look right down on the backs of the deer."

"There were dozens of them," Bob said. "The trails circled around the pond site and up into the cedar thickets. There were long lines of them, digging at the grass, jostling one another."

Bob and Joe looked at one another,

shook their heads, laughed, and shook their heads again before Joe started up again. "Bob, the darn fool, he has this idea. He wanted to ride on one of the deer, on the back of one of the bucks. He crouched on the edge of a cutting, about four feet or so above the deer. I went back aways and shooed two big bucks along toward where Bob was perched, ready to go, and when one was trotting by, Bob timed his jump and down he dropped, shoes and all."

"I landed just perfect," Bob interrupted. "Just perfect, right astraddle him."

He laughed again, reliving the feat. "Well sir that deer reared up on its hind legs, me on its back, and then planted both front hoofs, one on each side, right down through each of my snowshoes. Holy Lord, I couldn't fall off if I tried. Those front legs were clinched right through the webbing of my shoes. I was strapped on solid."

Joe continued, a serious look on his

face. "There was Bob going round and round those narrow trails. He went by me twice. I saw him grabbing to hang on. The deer had no mane, so I think he had him by the ears. Then the whole herd stampeded, and Bob disappeared into the cedars. I was certain that was the last I'd ever see of him."

"What happened?" Timothy's sister Rosalie asked. "Did you fall off? Were you trampled?"

"Don't worry, I made it back all right," Bob answered in a low voice, perhaps recalling the awful terror he'd felt. "The snow was less deep among the trees. I leaned a way forward, grasping desperately for something, anything, to hang onto. There was nothing. Then my shoes caught in the branches, first one, and then the other. They ripped loose and came off. I wasn't far behind. The toughest job was repairing the webbing so we could get home."

"Yes sir, leave it to Bob and his wild

ideas," Joe said. "That was always my job, getting Bob back home."

Bob changed the subject. "OK, where's that deck? I came to play cards!"

The kitchen table was set up with a kerosene lamp at one end and a bucket of russets at the other. Joe dealt out cards for Six Handed Auction, three against three. The bidding began timidly.

"Twenty."

"I'll hold."

"Make it."

"What is this? An old ladies' tea?" Bob demanded.

The next deal was more aggressive.

"Twenty," the bidder suggested.

"Twenty-five," Bob exploded.

"I'll hold it," the dealer answered.

"Thirty for sixty," Bob shot back.

"Make it," the dealer said, as Bob reached for the cat.

It was another great night of cards, Maritime style.

By late evening the apples had been eaten and the score was two games each, a good time to call it quits. Joe and Bob pulled on their coats and boots, lit the lantern, and trudged out to check the stock. The others trooped off to bed.

The next morning, Bob, all primed and fed, left to visit another lucky neighbour while Joe and the two boys packed a lunch and headed for the woodlot out on the ridge. It took many trees to heat a farmhouse through a long winter. The large hardwoods were felled with a crosscut, limbed with axes, and yarded with the horses. Great care was taken to protect the younger trees.

At noon they blanketed and fed the horses, then boiled fresh tea over a small fire, heated baked beans in a large frying pan, and thawed and toasted frozen sandwiches. It was only a matter of time until John posed the inevitable question: "What happened on that first try at finding the deer yard?"

The two boys and their father sat on two logs that angled out from the fire. The smoke swirled around their faces as they stretched their feet toward the coals. Joe, a cup of hot tea between his large hands, spoke slowly, choosing his words with care.

"It was a bit of a fluke, that accident, one of those strange things that often happen in the woods. It wasn't Bob's fault, but the poor guy would be there yet if he'd been alone. There were heavy rains all fall. The brooks overflowed and the swamps and low places were full of water. Then it turned cold. Twenty below zero for days before any snow came. There was ice everywhere. When the snow did come, it snowed and snowed.

"We were tramping along, Bob ahead breaking trail, while I followed a little way behind. We climbed down into a low swampy area. The going was good with snow higher than the alders. It was soft powdery snow too, not a bit crusty. Suddenly, Bob started to sink. It was the weirdest thing. He dropped clear out of sight with just his hat sitting there on the snow. There was probably five feet of water in that hollow in the fall, then thick ice, followed by deep snow. Eventually the water drained away in the bitter cold, leaving nothing to support the ice. It gave way like a trap door. Bob dropped clear to the bare ground, and the snow came in on top of him. He didn't even have time to raise his hands. He was pinned solidly, unable to move, snow melting down his neck, with a ton of ice and snow on top of each snowshoe. There he was, with each foot strapped to a snowshoe, unable to wiggle a toe. You know, it was the first time I ever heard Bob cry. He would swear, then cry, then swear something awful."

By now the fire had burned itself out. The lunch was gone, and it was getting cold. As the two boys gathered things together, Joe continued. "I cleared the snow from his face and Bob calmed down a little. Luckily the snow was fairly light and easy to move. I soon had his head uncovered and his hands free. Using my snowshoes for shovels, we dug and dug.

The stuff just kept falling back in. Finally, in that hole on my head, feet up in the air, I ran a knife along each of his legs and cut the straps free. We never did get those shoes out. What a time we had getting back home."

Joe stood up, breaking the spell. He stepped back from the log, stretched, and looked around. "What tree are we cutting next?"

"How 'bout that burly maple?" John suggested, getting up.

And soon they were all back to work.

2

MARY O'HALLORAN

The Johnville church was located on a low hill near the center of the community. The priest's house and barn sat nearby. Homes in the area were small and plain, but the large wooden church was a source of pride with its hand-carved altar, stained glass windows, and bright statues. The parishioners' faith had come from Ireland. Their allegiance to Irish culture and special devotion to the rosary were well known in the diocese.

Father Paul was fond of his devout parishioners. A tall, spare man used to physical work, he ensured his flock received the best spiritual care and assisted with their physical needs too. He attended barn raisings, pitched in at frolics, and raised a few cows of his own. He loved the small family farms with their rocky fields, so recently cleared from the forest with arduous toil, and he loved the people too, though it wasn't always clear to him whether they loved him back. Regardless, they made sure he was well looked after. The parish house he lived in was large. His driving horse, Molly, was easily the best around. He had running water, an indoor toilet, an attractive dining room, and a spacious living room. He even had a new wall telephone, a gadget few in the parish had ever seen.

One cold November evening he sat down to his housekeeper Mrs. Reilly's superb fare, the roast done to perfection, the vegetables cooked just right. "I sure appreciate the hot meal, Mrs. O'Reilly," he told her. "The drive today really gave me an appetite."

"I do my best, Father." Mrs. O'Reilly enjoyed working for the priest. She had had plenty of experience raising her own brood of seven. She was happy to be away from her domineering husband— her daughter-in-law could handle him. "The bitter cold makes us all extra hungry."

Father Paul enjoyed the meal, but he was tired. A tour of the south road had left him sad and confused. Most of the people he met were happy and content with their lot in life, but they were poor, and the lure of distant cities was strong. The sight of empty houses had disturbed him. He'd heard stories of men leaving home for work in factories, and of deserted families expecting money that never came. The difficult rural life made the strong stronger, but it only bled strength from the weak.

And the needless gossip, the sad, malicious tales—it troubled him, suggesting as it did a lack of sympathy for those less well off. Why couldn't people tend to their own sins, rather than worry about the imagined sins of others?

"Can I get you some more potatoes?" Mrs. O'Reilly asked. "Or would you prefer some hot rolls?"

Before Father Paul could answer, the phone rang—quite loud and startling in the big old house. Mrs. O'Reilly's face lit up at the sound. She loved answering the telephone, and usually knew every caller. It was nice to know who was phoning the priest.

She picked up the receiver, put it to her ear, and rose on her toes to speak timidly into the mouthpiece. "Hello?"

She listened briefly, then, looking puzzled, handed the receiver to Father Paul.

"Father, come quickly." The connection was poor—Father Paul couldn't tell if the voice he heard was that of a man or a woman. "It's young Mary O'Halloran, on the North Road, just across the Monquart bridge. She's sick. She needs you. She won't last until morning. She's asking for a priest. Please come as soon as you can." The voice faded into dial tone.

It was six miles by horse and buggy, over a dark cold road, to the Monquart stream and its covered bridge, and beyond that to the small cabin, which Father Paul knew to be a home to desperately sick women. Aware of the crude stories told about Mary O'Halloran, his heart went out to her. He knew the North Road women shunned her. He suspected her spiritual needs were as severe as her physical, but he'd been asked to help, not judge her.

"Please prepare my sick call kit while I fetch the buggy," he instructed Mrs. O'Reilly.

"Who is it, Father?" she asked.

"Mary O'Halloran," he told her. "I need to hurry."

He left for the barn.

Mrs. O'Reilly was sorry the meal had

been interrupted but thankful the priest had had time to eat at least a portion of it. As she checked the contents of his kit, especially the anointing oils, holy water, candles, and crucifix, she reflected upon Mary O'Halloran, who, she knew, hadn't been to church in years, and no wonder. Catching sight of the telephone, she wondered aloud, "Who placed the call?"

With the help of a small kerosene lantern Father Paul quickly harnessed Molly, his shiny black mare. The short rest and meal had refreshed them both. After retrieving his kit from the house, he made his way to the church, a short distance away. Lantern held high, he entered the church and removed a sacred host from the tabernacle and carefully placed it in a special pouch, which he hung around his neck. A sacred host, the body and blood of Christ, was an essential part of every sick call.

Back in the buggy, the lantern hanging from the back, the priest urged the young mare into a fast walk. Father

Paul loved cool fall evenings, when the sky overflowed with bright stars, but he worried about the dark road with its terrible bumps and numerous holes. Holes that could break a buggy wheel, or even snap a horse's leg. He felt a little better remembering that the full moon would rise soon.

The dirt road was narrow, twisty, and bordered by endless rail fences. After climbing a long, winding hill, the mare turned onto the North Road, where the farms were farther apart. Tall trees crowded together on either side of the road, blocking out the sky. Father Paul was afraid a wild animal might frighten his horse, but the faithful mare plodded forward unconcerned.

The last mile to the Monquart stream was mainly downhill. The full moon rose, bright over the trees, encouraging them onward. Father Paul heard running water and caught the dank smell of sedge grass and alders. Seconds later a large covered bridge loomed over horse and buggy, silhouetted against the moon.

Inside the bridge it was dark, though small apertures admitted some moonlight. Molly entered without hesitation, her steel shod hooves ringing on the plank floor. Bright moonlight illuminated the tunnel at the far end. As the priest watched, a large animal came into view, partially obscuring the light. It trotted toward them. Soon it was close enough for Father Paul to identify it as a black dog. But not just any dog. It was massive and possessed burning eyes that shone like live coals in the dull gloom. As it approached, it began to growl ominously, and then darted forward, barking viciously. Terrified, the mare reared up on its hind legs, slashing the air with her front hoofs. Father Paul leapt from the buggy and grabbed Molly's bridle to keep her from backing up and smashing the buggy into the bridge. The huge dog backed off, snarling. Father Paul realized that the creature's blazing eyes were riveted on the pouch on his chest, tracking its movements as it swung back and forth.

"The sacred host bothers you, doesn't it, big fellow?" he said, being careful to keep it in the dog's sight while trying desperately to keep Molly under control.

He reached for the holy water. Holding the host in one hand and the holy water in the other, he stepped toward the cowering beast. "This visit is important to you, isn't it? You want to frighten me away."

The dog seemed to increase in size. Its growl became louder and more menacing. Father Paul squirted a tiny stream of blessed water at the animal. The beast leapt sideways, twisting in terror trying to avoid it. When a few drops fell on its glossy fur, the beast howled and shrieked as though scalded in boiling oil. In two leaps it was gone. The covered bridge was empty except for a subdued priest, a badly shaken horse, and a new smell like that of burning sulphur.

With the path cleared, it only required a few minutes to cross the stream, climb a low hill, and reach the O'Halloran house. The small building was dark and cheerless. After leaving the loyal horse in a tiny lean-to at the back, Father Paul entered the only door, which led to a small kitchen. The place was ice cold. "Hello!" he called.

No one answered.

He crossed the kitchen and entered a small bedroom. A young woman was lying on a filthy bed. All alone, unassisted, without food or heat, she was close to death.

"Father," she whispered faintly when she saw him. "I knew you would come. I prayed, and I had lost all right to pray, but I did pray, I really prayed."

With the little strength she had left, the sick girl wept uncontrollably.

Afraid she would die at once, the priest tried to console her. "You have every right to pray. God will forgive your sins. Please allow me to hear your confession. Confessing your sins to me is to tell them directly to Christ himself."

There wasn't time to build a fire or look for food. He gave the exhausted girl communion, tendered the last rites, and stayed beside her until she passed away, at peace with herself and God.

After her soul departed, Father Paul gazed sadly upon the young face, reposed at last. He wondered how long it had been since she had eaten or been able to fuel the fire. "More sinned against than sinning," he whispered. "Our saviour would not allow you to die in sin. The Devil himself could not prevail against you."

He went outside to settle his restless horse, and to scrounge wood for the kitchen stove. He needed help to clean the house, lay out the body, and keep vigil for the night. He preferred not to risk the dark lonely road again before daylight, so he decided to call Mrs.

O'Reilly, to calm her worries and request help. However, without even looking, he knew. There was no phone.

"That's right," he murmured. "Not in this house. Not in this poverty."

The funeral was not well attended. The few who came heard a stirring sermon. Father Paul was eloquent. "Those who have everything on earth, what can they look forward to in heaven? A young woman allowed to starve in a land of plenty. Heaven was created for such as her. Last week she had nothing. Today she is clothed in glory."

A few weeks later, on a bitterly cold evening shortly before Christmas, a local farmer approached the Monquart stream just as the sun was setting. From his seat on the pung he could see the last rays of soft pink light reflecting from the river ice. A recent storm had left the snow piled deeply in open areas and the light pung bounced roughly over a frozen drift as it entered the covered bridge. The horse's feet rang loudly on the bare planks as the rugged farmer shivered uneasily, chilled from the cold, in spite of his thick coat and heavy sleigh blanket.

Gradually he became aware of a beautiful young woman sitting relaxed and serene beside him, her knees tucked under the blanket, her hands folded on her lap. She wore a thick cloth coat of gorgeous material. A brightly coloured bonnet covered her head, and an elegant scarf was wrapped about her neck and thrown back over her shoulder. When the farmer turned tremulously toward her, she glanced up at him, a radiant smile on her young face.

"A curious thing," he described later, "was her soft bare hands, which clutched a pearl rosary, her fingers indifferent to the cold."

When the sleigh quit the bridge, the girl vanished.

Traffic soon increased on the North Road. On Sundays, whole families often drove back and forth over the bridge, but no one saw anything out of the ordinary.

Stories soon spread. The local farmer had been a little drunk that day. Father Paul's dog became everything from a black sheep to a moose.

The day Mrs. Cronin found the slim, well-dressed young woman sitting beside her in the buggy she arrived home in shock, incapacitated for a week. When the renowned gossip finally spoke about the incident, it was the rich clothes and dainty rosary that fascinated her. "Why would the lovely daughter of someone so rich ever haunt the Monquart?" she was heard to ask.

Many different people saw the young girl. They were always alone, usually in a sleigh or buggy. The apparition would appear suddenly, sitting alongside them as they entered the bridge, only to vanish as they exited.

Ed Corbett was in a bad mood one warm night in June. A girl had rebuffed him at a house party, and he'd been drinking. When the heavenly creature appeared beside him, his groping hands found only empty air when he glommed for her.

Nobody ever moved into the small cabin or took care of it. Within a few years it fell into ruin. A new owner had it torn down, the debris burned, and the basement levelled. A crop of clover grew over the site of the cabin, followed by potatoes and grain. When all sign of the cabin's existence disappeared, so too did the mysterious sightings at the covered bridge.

3

FENCING

The job of fencing is seldom popular on a farm. My dad usually left the stringing of fences to rainy days, or at least days too wet for anything else. He didn't question their necessity. Good fences make good neighbours, was a popular saying among farmers. Nobody appreciates having their neighbour's cattle run amok in their oat fields. Anyhow, for some strange reason, I loved fencing.

Timing is also an important aspect of farm life. The last load of hay was in our barn only minutes before the rain started.

The warm shower came just in time to revitalize our front pasture and jump start the grass in the newly mown hayfields. We could now move our young stock to the back field, leaving the milk cows close to the house, where they'd be handy for milking. All that was needed was a nice fence across the back field. During the night the rain moved on. The next day was dry enough for fencing and too wet for anything else. Dad was up early, eager to get started.

While Bill and I milked the cows, Dad and Ambrose harnessed the horses and loaded the wagon. They never bothered to remove the hay rack, just loaded it with page wire, crowbars, axes, saws, staples, and what few stakes they could find. Bill and I finished the milking just in time to climb aboard, where we relaxed perched high atop the pile of stakes as the faithful horses plodded toward the back field.

Mom promised to have the girls bring sandwiches out to the spring for lunch.

This looked to be a great day, a family day. Maybe that's why I liked fencing so much.

Our first stop was a cedar swamp to supplement our supply of stakes. Ambrose and Dad cut and trimmed the small cedar trees while Bill and I lugged them out to the field. Each stake was held with one end on a stump while someone sharpened them with an axe. They looked like big, overgrown pencils.

Finally, well supplied, we reached the back field where high timothy had waved in the breeze only days before. This field sat at the very back of our cleared land, set against a steep hill covered with tall trees, a thick forest that went on for miles. Our back field was the end of nowhere. From here we couldn't see any neighbours or hear any traffic. Only the distant sound of a train whistle, faintly heard on damp days, told us we were not alone in the world.

Dad positioned the corner post carefully. Sighting on a distant tree to keep the fence straight, he stepped off five paces. I punched the first hole with a crowbar. Bill set a stake in place and Ambrose drove it down solidly with a big wooden mallet. It was a leisurely day for the work horses. It was hard work for us. We took our time, alternating from job to job. Dad appreciated each hole we dug or mallet we swung. We were happy to be useful.

A long narrow valley stretched out from the neighbouring hills, jutting into our farm. A small brook rippled noisily down its center. Tall trees provided shade. A steep cliff formed a border between the field we were fencing and the valley floor. A spring, clear and cold, bubbled into a small pool that had formed at the base of the cliff, then flowed toward the brook, less than fifty feet away. A narrow path, its upper end hidden behind some small firs, slashed diagonally downward as it led from the field where we worked toward the enticing pool.

The pleasant work made the time pass quickly. Shortly before noon we saw the girls approaching with our lunch. I offered to fetch a bucket of drinking water from the spring. I grabbed a pail from the wagon and started down over the cliff. The path was seldom used and the footing treacherous. I wondered who had first marked it out, as the path seemed to have been dug directly from the face of the cliff. To my right, on the inside of the path, the bank rose almost straight up, while a sheer drop loomed on my left. A red squirrel perched on top of a tall spruce only a few feet away. I filled the pail at the spring, then reclined by the side of an ancient stump, enjoying the coolness of the glade after the heat of the open field. The huge brown stump seemed out of place among the many healthy trees surrounding it.

I returned with the drinking water to a very relaxed scene. The horses had been turned loose to graze. My older sister, Marion, very feminine in a flowery white dress, was spreading out sandwiches on a cloth laid upon the grass. She also had a large potato salad and a thermos of tea. A huge maple provided lots of shade. I sat on the grass next to Toby, our big yellow dog, just across from Dad who had adjusted the wagon tongue for a seat. Only the occasional stomping of the horses' feet and swishing of their tails at an errant fly competed with the crickets and the birds.

"What's going on at the house?" Dad asked, breaking the silence.

Marion knelt on the grass on the other side of Toby, unconcerned about stains on her dress, and even less concerned about the house. "Nothing," she said.

"The path to the spring, why's it worn like that?" I asked, fishing for a story.

"Yes," Ambrose added. "We never allow the cattle down there. Who dug it out like that?"

Dad looked past the horses toward

the newly mown field, and we knew that he'd taken the bait. Ambrose grinned at me. Someone threw Toby a crust of bread, and Dad started talking.

"Over a hundred years ago this was the site of a lumber camp. Look, you can see the outline of some buildings just over there." Dad pointed beyond where the horses were grazing.

Sure enough, now that our attention had been drawn to it, we could see a faint rectangular impression in the ground.

"The bunkhouse was right there. The cookshack was just across from it, and the stables were just back of them both. Your grandfather had a real mess to clean up when he cleared this field. At first, the men had no idea what it was. They found a bunch of second growth, the trees all thick and brambly, then noticed rotten logs, a stone foundation, old jugs and broken dishes. They even found axe heads and broken chains."

"There was forest everywhere then,"

Ambrose remarked. "Why would lumbermen travel this far up the river?"

"They were after pine for mast and spars," Dad said. "Scouts searched the whole country for tall, straight pine. The sailing ships needed so many. This area had beautiful pine. The lumber crews cut them all, just left us the stumps. What a job we had clearing those stumps from the fields. Pine takes years to rot. We often used dynamite. The stumps are still in the gully. They cut a lot of pine along that brook.

"The main depot and piling yards were at Florenceville, there on that big flat by the river. The hauling was done on winter sled roads that tried to follow the streams. The road from here followed our brook to the Branch, on down to the Hawke, which flowed into the river just above Florenceville. Horses can only move heavy loads on the downhill, or perhaps on the level. Isn't that right, George?" Dad looked fondly at our big red workhorse, who paid him no mind.

"The cook was an older man. His wife and grandson helped him. They moved into the cookshack as soon as the ground was frozen and supplies could be hauled in. The buildings were made from rough logs. They were put together in the summer, while other crews chopped the roads out." Dad looked at me. "The boy's name was Tommy, same as yours, and he was only your age too. Tommy slept in the bunkhouse with the men. He was proud of that, sleeping with the men. Tommy's main jobs were fetching water from the spring, chopping firewood, and caring for the horses.

"He worked hard at the camp, and his Granddad never allowed him to go to the depot on weekends. The entire crew often left at noon on Saturday, all piled onto a couple of supply sleds, pulled by the best teams. There at the main camp they met men from other areas. They ate, drank, sang, and really had a great time. The cook never left the camp, said he was too old for that foolishness. At least he had a break from cooking. Tommy had to feed, water and care for the rest of the horses. He led them, one by one, down the path to the spring. Then he cleaned the stables, put out fresh bedding, and strapped a warm blanket on each horse for the night.

"One weekend in February, with the snow deep and drifted, but with the bitter cold of January over, the crew left for the depot as usual. It was a little after one on Saturday that they left, and it was about five on Sunday when they straggled back. The men, tired and hung over, were hungry as wolves and looking forward to a hot dinner.

"The foreman burst into the cookshack yelling, 'we're back!' Only to find the place in shambles—the fire out, furniture smashed, the cupboards ripped down, and the cook and his wife both dead, lying in pools of blood, both bludgeoned to death. The young boy, Tommy, was gone, no sign of him anywhere. When the driver entered the stables, he found the horses restless, unfed, their blankets all tangled, definitely uncared for. The entire camp was in a sorry state.

"The men were in a state of shock, completely sober by now. They were fond of Tommy and fervently hoped he had no part in this. But then, where was he? And who could have killed the helpless old couple? There was only the cold dark forest all around.

"Eventually Tommy crawled out from under a huge bushy pine top, half frozen, delirious, and terrified. He had no winter boots, mitts, or cap on. One of the men carried him up the path and into the cookshack. By now a hot fire was blazing and the place was starting to warm up. Some men were cleaning up the place and trying to start dinner.

"Hot soup, a warm blanket, the fire, and lots of attention gradually brought Tommy around. Luckily, he was wearing woollen underwear and thick pants. Men in log cabins seldom undress at bedtime in winter; they usually put more clothes on."

Dad took a break in his story to fill his mug with hot tea. Ambrose shot me a sly glance. Dad's story could delay work by another half an hour. Best of all, the story was a good one. All that activity on our own back field, the tail end of nowhere.

"Could Tommy tell them what happened?" Marion asked anxiously.

"'I took good care of the horses, honest I did,' Tommy told them," Dad said. "The old man had given him the lantern last evening, so he checked everything, the stables, the horses, the blankets, and even fed them more hay. Then he came back to the bunkhouse, put a big stick on the fire, pulled his boots off, blew out the light, and crawled into his bunk. He was asleep in no time. It was so quiet. Then he woke up. There was someone screaming. Then he heard another man, not anyone he ever knew. 'Where did you hide it?' the man yelled.

'Saving it for your old age, are you? You'll never see any old age, you bastard.'

"Tommy was terrified. What if they came looking in the bunkhouse? He slipped down to the floor. His coat was on a hook near the window. It was almost morning. In the faint light, he could just make out a figure at the cookshack door. There was loud shumping and bumping and smashing inside. Oh God, what should he do? He had to think. He knew someone was in the shack, beating his grandparents up, and tearing the place apart. He wanted to get outside, to hide, and that lookout was watching. He pulled on his coat, no time to look for boots or mitts. The only door faced the cookshack, only yards away across the frozen snow.

"'Please don't let them see me,' he prayed, and pushed the door gently outward. The metal hinges squeaked loudly in the morning quiet. He dashed outside, swung around the corner, and plunged desperately down the icy path, his sock feet bruising on the frozen hoof tracks. It was still dark in the gully. Thinking quickly, he ran past the spring, up a tote trail by the brook and crawled beneath a pine top. Daylight came slowly as the sun climbed over the high hills. The eastern sky glowed with a soft red, the frost glittered sharply on the snow, then he saw two men feel their way carefully down the steep path. He saw them stop by the spring and search the ground carefully for tracks. He fervently hoped the frozen snow, packed by the horses' hooves and torn by pine logs would provide few clues. Angry and agitated, they stomped up the trail, only feet from Tommy, as he crouched motionless under the bushy pine top. He could see them clearly. They both wore heavy coats, and one, a real big guy, carried an axe in his right hand, and wore a leather cap with floppy ear covers. The smaller man had a club, a handle of some sort, and wore a knit cap. It had a red tassel dangling from it. They stared right at him, or something near him. Tommy never moved an eyelash. He was so close. He saw them so clearly, surely they could see him. Then their gaze moved back and forth as their eyes searched the scattered brush piles.

"'Come out,' the big man yelled. 'We won't harm you. We only want the money. Tell us where that old bugger hid it.'

"Up and down the gully they tramped, past huge stumps and messy brush piles, their heavy boots crunching the snow and their frozen breath trailing in the frosty air. Tommy could see their shaggy beards, hear them cursing and complaining. He'd know them anywhere."

Dad, his weather-beaten face relaxed in a smile, paused for another sip of tea. In his soiled hat, bib overalls and leather work boots he looked like a regular farmer, not a storyteller, but he sure held the attention of this group.

I stared down into the gully, seeing

young Tommy, just my age, the frost penetrating his sock feet and bare hands, as he gazed terrified at the two assassins stalking him. *Won't harm me indeed*, he must have thought bitterly. I looked across the peaceful hay field, noisy with crickets while it soaked up the hot sun: a cookshack, bunkhouse, stables, and a double murder, wow!

The horses browsed the short grass, the dog slept, and the fence wire lay untouched.

"Did the men get caught?" Marion asked impatiently.

Ambrose smiled as he looked at his watch. Bill and I were all ears.

"When they couldn't find Tommy, the two killers left on snowshoes," Dad said. "Went right through the woods there on the other side of the gully. They crossed the river on the ice about ten miles above the depot. It was easy to track them. They crossed into Maine. The Sheriff at the Fort arrested them, and they were tried in Fredericton. Tommy described them perfectly, they had the cook's watch with them, and witnesses claimed to have seen them at the depot hanging around asking questions. One of them had known the cook at a camp on the Miramichi. The cook had always been a talker, had claimed he was saving money for his old age, that he and the missus were retiring in Saint John.

"It was all talk. They never saved a cent. They were killed for nothing. The killers were hung, both of them, in Fredericton. My old aunt told me about it. She was there, but she didn't go to the execution. She and her family came up the river on a barge that summer."

We must have finished the fence, but I don't remember for sure. The terrified boy, though, and my Dad sitting there on the wagon tongue, drinking his tea, keeping us all enthralled... well, I'll never forget that.

4

MY FATHER'S FARM

On my Father's farm
>I was lost and alone
My older brothers
All outshone me
One by one,
They all left home.
My father and I the only ones left.
I didn't measure up.
But then,
I never cared a bit!

5

A SMALL FLAT STONE

The family was poor.

There was little money for their father's burial.

The tombstone was a small flat stone with the name and date carefully carved on the front.

Some years later the son came home to visit the grave site. He took one look

and said this won't do.

He pulled out a fat wallet and ordered a new stone.

One bigger and better.

They threw the old one over the fence

Soon to be covered with bushes.
It became the front doorstep of a
nearby house.
The right size and shape,
and with the name on the bottom,
who would know the difference?
Well everybody.

6

TOBY THE FARM DOG

Toby was a big yellow farm dog. Fetching the cows at milk time was Toby's main love in life. As soon as he heard us whistle or rattle a milk pail, he would come on the tear. We would call, and that big dog would spring to his feet in the kitchen, run for the door, leap across the porch, and literally tear around the end of the house as he headed for the pasture. If any Holstein needed her milk warmed, they had only to fool around with our dog, Toby, and that cow's milk supply was soon ready for hot toddies. I was very proud of Toby.

Unfortunately, Dad lacked our fondness for Toby. He seldom missed a chance to tell us the dog was useless, that Toby never knew which end of a cow to chase. Dad said all Toby did was bark, that he wouldn't know what to do with a cow if he ever caught one. Of course, Dad was right, but we never cared. We wanted Toby to be a circus dog. We taught him tricks. We had that dog jumping through hoops, hauling snow sleds, and catching balls. The proper handling of cows took second place.

We loved our big yellow dog, and I'm sure every cow gave us greater respect when Toby was around. They were much less likely to step in the pail or bat us on the head with a filthy tail.

I'm not entirely sure how it happened that hot July day. Bill, my younger brother, threw the ball, and I guess I must have missed it. The ball went smashing through the porch window, scattering broken glass clear across the kitchen floor. Bill and I spent an hour cleaning up the mess. It was our favourite kitchen window. On wet days we stared out at the rain beating down on the porch railing. On fine days we stood on the porch staring in at the dinner preparations. It was a typical farmhouse window, with four large panes of glass, all carefully puttied in. Bill and I took out all the broken glass and cleared away the old putty.

When Dad came for supper, he said there wasn't time to go into town for a new pane. Said everyone was too busy with the haying. He didn't think we would freeze in July, and said that someone would go for glass the next rainy day.

I decided to teach Toby to jump through the broken window. I was looking in to check on supper, and there was the dog sleeping under the kitchen table. It was only natural to call Toby to say hello. So now there he was, with his nose in the opening, and one thing led to another. At first the dog was a little timid. I had to coax him with cookies and bacon rinds. First thing we knew, Toby jumped through that broken window as though jumping through a hoop. He came to his feet from under the table, made a flying leap, and out through the window he went. I would call to him, or just rattle a milk pail, and out Toby would come. I never even opened the door. A week went by with Toby jumping in and out of the window every day.

Mother complained about the broken window. It couldn't have been the cold, not with the hot weather we were having. It must have been the flies, especially with the cream separator in the corner of the kitchen. There's nothing worse than milk to attract swarms of house flies.

Toward the end of the week, with the hay slackened off, Dad told my older brother, Ambrose, to drive into town and buy a pane of glass. By four in the afternoon Ambrose was back. By five the window was fixed. I happened by just as my brother expertly smoothed out the putty.

"Well, you were a big help," Ambrose told me, stepping back to admire his handiwork. "You might at least round up the cows so we can start the milking."

Feeling a little guilty for not helping with the window, I immediately called for Toby. "Here Toby, old boy, come on, let's fetch those ornery cows." I rattled a milk pail for extra emphasis.

The instant I heard the dog's feet scrape the floor beneath the kitchen table I realized my error. With a flying leap, sixty pounds of speeding dog hit the new pane like a ton of bricks. It never even slowed Toby down. He landed on the porch amid a shower of glass, tore around the corner of the house, and headed for the pasture. I tore along right after him. It seemed, about then, a great time for rounding up cows.

7

SHUGRO HILL

It was a pleasant September day. The warmth of the afternoon sun had started to wane. Timothy had left the house early in the morning wearing a heavy jacket. By noon he'd been forced to strip down to shirt sleeves. The combination of hard work and hot sun had just been too much. Another one of the hazards of potato harvesting, dressing for the extremes of weather.

When Timothy felt that first evening chill, he glanced to the west, toward Mars hill, and noticed that the sun was sinking quickly. The shortness of

September days bothered him. He knew that fall evenings never produced the lingering twilight of June, but rather a swift and heavy darkness.

He grabbed the heavy basket he'd just filled and gently dumped the potatoes into a wooden barrel. Standing still, empty basket in hand, he carefully searched the nearby fields for wildlife, especially deer. This was hunting season, and little moved on the small farm that Timothy's keen eyes didn't see. The brilliant foliage surrounding him he took for granted, as familiar as fresh country air.

His sister Rosalie approached. "Will you empty these for me?"

Timothy lifted Rosalie's heaping basket easily. "We'll need to hurry with these last two rows before Dad comes back with the wagon."

Timothy would be sixteen in October, his birthday only three weeks away. Rosalie had turned fifteen in August. Timothy knew she really enjoyed those few weeks when she was only one year younger than him.

After two full days of work, the small field was still far from harvested. The untouched rows stretched away for yards, their withered tops leaving the grey soil bare and unprotected. A line of half-filled barrels stood along the two freshly dug rows, each a basket full apart.

Timothy and Rosalie started at the bottom of the field, eager to finish the last two rows of the day. Slowly they worked their way up the gradual slope. The horse-drawn digger had shaken most of the dirt from the potatoes. Still, they pawed into the soft soil and heavy sods with gloved hands, making sure they found every potato, stooping to grab them from the ground and piling them into soft Indian-made baskets. When their backs ached, they dropped to their knees and crawled along, dragging the baskets after them. A barrel held four full baskets. The previous two rows had half-filled them. Now, when they came to each barrel, Timothy emptied both baskets, filling the barrel up.

"There's Dad now," Rosalie shouted, just as they finished the two rows.

The horses seemed to sense the day's work was ending. The heavy farm wagon moved swiftly up the field. Timothy and Rosalie's father held the reins loosely in his left hand and scattered empty barrels with his right. Timothy met the wagon at the top of the field, after his father had turned the team around. Together they loaded the full barrels, Timothy lifting with his left hand, his Dad with his right. Afterward Timothy climbed onto the wagon and rolled the barrels into place. This was the part of potato harvesting that Timothy enjoyed the most. Here he stood, shoulder to shoulder with his father, lifting his share of the load.

After the last barrel was lifted into place Rosalie and their father headed home. It was tough going for the horses as the heavy load cut deep gouges into the soft field. Timothy watched until he saw the wagon lurch onto the main trail and smoother going.

After seeing them safely on their way, Timothy ran to a nearby tree where he'd left his rifle. It was fall, a time of colour and excitement. If he hurried, and with a little luck, he might still be able to bag a deer at Shugro Hill before dark. He carefully shoved five shells into the magazine. It was a 45-70 Winchester, an 1890 model, old but still lethal.

He walked quickly from the potato field, carrying the loaded rifle with care. He knew the deer sheltered in the thick woods during the day, coming out at dusk for their evening meal.

When he reached the line fence, he poked the rifle through first, then easily climbed through after it. Page wire, with its large rectangular openings, was easy to negotiate.

The Shugro field was badly neglected, full of tall weeds and wild grass. After having been abandoned it had re-seeded itself slowly and was now thick with tiny white spruce and a scattering of poplar. The rough field sloped upwards toward a dense wood. The closer Timothy came to this thin strip of forest—beyond which lay another small clearing, an old cellar, and apple trees—the more excited he became.

Just short of the tree line, Timothy stopped to catch his breath and look around. Long dark shadows already extended across Shugro field and over into the potato field where he'd toiled through the day. The hardwood ridges were still bright and colourful as they caught the last rays of the sinking sun.

Once rested, Timothy started toward the forest edge again. His heartbeat quickened. A shiver passed through him as he entered the tangled growth. His grip on the ancient Winchester tightened as he shredded his way closer to his favourite hunting spot. Once the site of the old Shugro house, which had long since rotted into the cellar, today it was home to burdocks, raspberry bushes and racoons. Tonight, it might be home to a fat deer. Dad would be surprised and proud, and the potato harvest would be much easier with fresh meat on the table.

The sun finally disappeared but Timothy didn't worry. It was the time of day when the deer came out to feed. Minutes later he was peering over a six-foot-high split rail fence bordering the Shugro clearing. Straight out from the fence, less than one hundred yards away, was a dark mass of raspberry bushes. Timothy could see the remains of the crumbling cellar, all that was left of the ancient Shugro house. A little to the right were the apple trees. Timothy's eyes searched the orchard carefully. His breath came fast, and his heart fairly pounded. Something moved, something big and black, he was certain. The day was darker than he'd expected. Darn these short days anyway. He'd have to cross the fence and try to work his way closer.

The fence was shaky, too rickety to

climb. Timothy wormed his way between two cedar rails and crawled carefully toward a small spruce tree. There, crouched behind the bushy tree, Timothy hoped to see what animal was enjoying the apples without being seen in return. He rose to one knee, the rifle thrust forward, and cautiously peered past the sheltering spruce. In the gathering dusk he received his first view of his intended victim. It was not the big peaceful buck he'd wished for. It was a large black bear, and it was coming straight toward him. The bear ambled along on all fours, carelessly moving through the tall, uncut grass, its huge head angled slightly upward as it sniffed the air for strange scents.

Another cold shiver climbed uninvited up Timothy's spine. His heart almost stopped from the shock. A quick prayer crossed his lips. He gripped his rifle tighter and thanked God for the meagre protection of the tiny tree. Less than fifty feet away the bear sensed danger. The hunter was downwind but gusts of cool air, bouncing around in the clearing, must have carried the human scent toward him.

A man's scent means big trouble for bears. Deep-rooted instincts warned the bruin to make tracks away from there. The scent was fleeting as the air currents shifted about. A bear's nose is sensitive, but its eyes are notoriously weak. The bear stopped its advance and fidgeted about, swinging its head from side to side. To aid its sight, and in a vain effort to locate the danger, it reared up on its hind legs and stared straight ahead.

As the bear rose to its full height, Timothy's mouth fell open and his eyes glazed with fright. The bear stood in the tiny clearing swinging its front legs like hairy arms, its huge head silhouetted against the sky, its size sufficient to intimidate veteran hunters. Young Timothy, crouched in the shadow of his bushy spruce, was petrified.

If that ugly brute moves one step closer, he thought desperately, *I'll let him have it.*

The bear sniffed the air. It swung its huge head about. Apparently satisfied that there was no danger, it dropped to all fours and trotted rapidly closer, heading straight toward Timothy, and into great danger.

Timothy watched the huge bear rapidly close in on him and wondered how he'd managed to get into this predicament. He pulled back the hammer and sighted for the bear's swiftly advancing shiny eyes. The steel hammer clicked loudly in the still night air. With a loud snort, the bear stopped its approach, then rose to show its broad chest to the young hunter.

Now's the time, Timothy thought grimly.

He squeezed the trigger.

Flame and lead poured from the barrel. A terribly loud bang reverberated across the narrow clearing. Timothy was only faintly aware of the sound as the rifle's violent kick drove him backwards.

His father had just unhitched the horses when he heard the shot boom and echo up on the hill. He wondered if the young lad was having any luck.

Timothy heard a piercing scream and a blood curdling roar as the frightened bear, his shoulder ripped by the heavy slug, dashed at full speed toward the rail fence. The wounded animal passed only feet from where the farm boy knelt unseen. With a desolate cry it leapt to clear the fence only to land on the top rail. Grabbing desperately with its claws, the bear fell backwards to the ground, bringing a tangle of rails with it. With another mournful wail the wounded beast leapt again, easily clearing what was left of the fence. In a second it was out of sight, disappearing among the trees.

Panic-stricken, Timothy bolted across the clearing, covering the same ground the bear had, but in the opposite direction. It was completely dark now. Feet flying, gripping the rifle tightly, the brush tearing at his clothes, Timothy ran recklessly into the blackness. Gradually he calmed down, his breath coming in gasps. Unsure where he was going, or where to step on the rough ground, he stopped. Slowly, he turned in the thick darkness to gaze back the way he had come.

Why, that poor bear was just as frightened as I was.

After careful consideration, he decided on the safest route home, certain of one thing only: that it would not be the direction the poor bear had taken.

8

THE LOG DRIVE

Loud shouts and heavy footsteps roused Bob Tucker from deep sleep. He awoke to the faintest hint of daylight.

"Up! Up!" a rough voice said. "Hurry! We have logs to move. The cook's waiting if you want to eat."

Bob pushed the blankets back from his face and felt the cold morning air pour over him. A large man in a heavy parka carrying a kerosene lantern strode the length of the bunkhouse. The feeble yellow light did little to illuminate the outlines of men slowly coming to life. Bob grabbed his woollen pants from the foot of the bunk and quickly stepped into them. He pulled on his rubber boots, thick cloth jacket, warm farm cap, and joined the crew headed out into the frosty April morning.

The sun peeked over the eastern hills with a sudden burst of light, bathing the immense forest, winding river and small clearing in pinkish white light. The crew, fortified by a hearty breakfast of bacon, ham, pancakes, fried potatoes and black coffee, lined up outdoors waiting for orders. Bob viewed the quiet scene with an experienced eye. As a veteran of numerous camps on the Tobique and Miramichi rivers, the rough log buildings with their tar paper roofs surrounded by huge piles of newly cut logs were not new to him. He had often heard how they did things differently in Maine. It all appeared the same to him.

The foreman, a rugged, heavy-set individual, soon had everyone loaded onto supply sleds rigged up with two plank seats and pulled by two Morgan horses. The men sat four to a row facing each other, equipment piled on the floor between them. The foreman waited until all the sleds were loaded, then climbed onto Bob's, joining the driver on the high seat up front. The lead team pulled out first with the others following in line. They passed the stables and swung around behind the log piles, affording the men a clear view of the river. The water ran high with the spring freshet. Broken chunks of ice moved along in the fast current.

The steel runners of Bob's sled crunched loudly on the frozen ice and snow of the log road, but Bob knew the melting would begin again as soon as the sun climbed higher in the cloudless sky. The sled bounced over a snow-packed trail, a narrow cutting chopped through heavy woods that followed along the right-hand side of the river. The horses never slowed as the awkward sled teetered up and down over cradle knolls, stumps, and frozen lumps of ice, all the while twisting around numerous large trees. The river passed in and out of view as it meandered first one way then another. It was nowhere in sight when the driver pulled hard on the reins, slowly bringing the fresh and spirited horses to a stop.

"All right, Bob, this is where we get off." The foreman's voice sounded unnaturally loud in the quiet of the forest.

The other workers gave Bob the once over, taking in his wide shoulders, stocky build, broad young face and short black beard. They noted his heavy warm clothes, not unlike their own, fairly standard winter wear.

One of the older men chuckled softly. "I think you're getting the rock there, son."

The foreman smiled slightly. "Don't worry. The rock won't be a problem for Bob. He's run the Miramichi."

Bob searched his new boss's face for a touch of sarcasm. He discerned none.

The foreman and the whole crew seemed to show real respect.

"Grab some tools from the pile there," the foreman said. "And don't forget some lunch."

Bob dropped a bundle of sandwiches from a bucket into a side pocket and carefully picked out a spiked pole and a double bitted axe. He followed the older man down a path in the snow that led toward the river. The distance was greater than expected because the river, on one of its wild swings, had moved sharply to the east and then cut back to the west creating an oxbow. About twenty feet from shore, straight out from the point, Bob saw a flat grey shape sticking up out of the water.

"The rock," he muttered, recalling the ominous laugh of the man in the sled.

He studied the dark sullen waters streaming past the isolated point, carefully surveyed the gigantic rock anchored like a boat offshore, and felt just a little apprehensive. When he turned back around, though, and met the foreman's penetrating gaze, he was careful not to allow his concerns to show.

"Anyone who can handle this area gets paid extra," the foreman told him. "Anyone who can keep the logs moving past that rock."

It had been a hard winter. Work had been scarce. Bob thought about his wife and young children at home. He needed the job and the extra money. Both men looked at the rock, at how its upstream point split the current. They both knew how quickly the logs could pile up against that point, log on top of log, until the whole river was blocked, bringing the whole drive to a stop until some fearless river-man used dynamite to break up the jam.

"Just keep the logs moving and the job's mine, is that what you're saying?" Bob asked.

"Until the drive's over, and extra pay for doing it," the foreman assured him.

They shook hands. The foreman left

Bob alone with the river and the gloomy forest, the river flowing dark and swift as the land released its burden of winter snow.

The first logs to float past were fairly scattered. A number floated by between the shore and the rock without touching either one. Then a big spruce butt scraped the gravelly point and ground to a halt. Bob pushed it free with his pole and watched it glide slowly down the river out of sight. He knew the river-men used the first logs dumped in the river to bridge rough spots. Logs were chained end to end to create booms to steer the main drive past rock ledges, alder swamps, bogans, dead waters and the like where jams often started. There was no way to prepare his rock for the deluge that he knew was coming.

By mid-morning the crew at the yard was dumping logs into the river faster. Runners on horseback monitored the situation, riding up and down the river, working out any kinks to allow the real drive to begin in earnest. One runner discovered Bob out on the rock, his feet braced well apart for better balance, carefully guiding stray logs past with his long pole.

"Any problems out there?" the man on horseback yelled.

"Nothing I can't handle," Bob answered cheerfully.

"Heck, you're not even wet! How'd you manage to get out there?"

"Oh, I just rode a log over. Plenty around, don't you think?"

"Good man! Keep it up. You're doin' fine." The runner jerked his horse around, dashed quickly up the narrow snow-covered path, and disappeared out of sight, leaving Bob alone with the river again.

The water splashed and gurgled with the current. Crows cawed loudly overhead. Bob heard traffic on the main trail just out of sight, but nobody else ventured down the path toward his lonely post.

At noontime the logs slacked off. Maybe the yard crew broke for lunch, or word came from downstream to ease up. Bob never knew. He took advantage of the break to ride a log over to shore for his lunch. The sandwiches tasted fine, but they were cold and not nearly enough. Having expected a hot lunch to be delivered, he was disappointed. He was determined to have something better the next day.

Soon he was back at work. The action was picking up. He noticed a large log floating crossways in the current, heading directly his way, with a whole tangle of others right behind it. If it struck the rock dead center it could be trouble. He leapt outward, landing lightly on the crossways log just as it fetched up. It rolled under his feet and bounced in the water. Unconcerned for his safety and footing, Bob drove into the tangled logs coming behind. With sheer strength and agility, he pushed a great many out into mid-stream. Then, with a tremendous heave, he pushed his bucking log and the rest of the jam toward the inside channel. Shoving and pushing, he coaxed them downstream, and jumped clear of the logs back onto the big rock, ready to do battle again before they floated by the lower end. It was the closest call of his first day. He was concerned about the days to come when the yard crew would really start dumping logs in.

Early on that first day, about mid-afternoon, the yard crew stopped work early. It would take until dark to clear the lower river out. This allowed Bob to be one of the first men back at the cook shack for supper. One day over and his feet were still dry. He felt proud as he sat down to a hearty meal of pot roast, baked potatoes, hot rolls and biscuits. It was the best meal he'd eaten since killing the moose in the fall.

After dinner, Bob had his first chance to really look the camp over. He wasn't alone. Milder temperatures and increased daylight enticed the men to wander about. There wasn't much to see, just a small camp in the woods, but the men quietly inspected the horse stables, hay barns, workshops, and supply depots.

By seven the next morning the logs were rolling past the rock on both sides. Bob knew he was in for a tough day. He was determined to fight it out, though. He pretended to be Horatio, holding the bridge against all comers, pushing away all logs that came near. But as the morning advanced, the logs came thicker and thicker.

"What are they doing?" he yelled to the surrounding forest. "Don't they know the river can't take it? That'll plug it solid!"

The logs came in great bunches, sideways, crossways, giving Bob no time to anticipate or plan ahead.

"It's brains not muscle that does the work," he muttered, heaving with all his might. "The current has to work for you, not against you."

At noon, tired and hungry, he looked longingly toward his lunch on the riverbank. Peering up-river, at the hundreds of logs pouring around the bend, he knew he couldn't leave his post. They would sweep around the point, slam into the big rock, and block the river in minutes. There would be no breaks, not for him, not even for the call of nature. *Where are the runners?* he wondered. Even a few minutes to eat, rest, climb off the rock and sit would be enough to renew his strength. He heard horses running, sleds squealing, and shouts coming from the trail, but no one ventured out to where one lone man struggled valiantly on.

He had one hope. The inept, inexperienced yard crew were dumping logs in too quickly, too bunched up. The river was too full. It had to jam somewhere, bringing the entire drive to a grinding halt. Bob struggled on, determined the jam would happen downstream from him. He stood on the rock, feet braced, tired and hungry, pushing logs to the right and to the left.

"Keep the logs moving and the job's yours," the foreman had told him.

Bob spied a mass of logs tangled into a raft as solid as though tied together. The mass slammed crossways into his rock. He looked upstream, apprehensive. The head of the tangle swung toward shore, where it blocked the inner channel completely.

Stupid buggers, Bob thought bitterly. *I should just walk to shore over those logs, eat my lunch, and let them go to hell!*

Instead he leapt onto the nearest log and jumped and ran from log to log until he reached the upstream head of the heavy jam. He had to keep it from enlarging. He treated the floating tangle the same as the tip of the rock, setting his feet solidly and pushing log after log out into the main stream. Still they kept coming on. He lost track of time as he leapt, shoved and pushed. Gradually, prying logs loose and setting them adrift, he gained headway, and the raft of logs grew smaller.

He tried desperately to work his way closer to the big rock, his main work platform, but never made it. A log began to spin beneath his feet. Another heavy timber, moving fast in the swollen current, struck it broadside. Bob's end of the log jerked upstream like a giant pry. The twist and sharp rotation tossed Bob high in the air, flipping him head-first into the icy water. His heavy clothes pulled him under the surface. Logs closed in above him. Heavy boots and gloves made swimming impossible. He crawled along the rough river bottom, under the careening logs, emerging breathless and badly shaken at the lower, protected end of the flat rock.

Shocked, half-frozen and overwhelmed, Bob clung to the rock's edge sucking in deep breaths. As he did so, he noticed a deep cleft in the rock: the beginning of a crack. He climbed out of the water, onto the rock, and noticed something else too.

The logs had stopped coming.

He crawled cautiously over the logs to the shore, pulled on a dry coat left there since early morning, and hurried along the path toward the main trail. Luckily, a teamster headed into camp saw the soaking, half-frozen figure and picked him up.

"It's jammed up solid down river," the driver explained. "They sent me for more dynamite. It'll be past midnight before the river-men blast all those logs out."

Dry clothes, a solid meal, a two-hour nap and Bob was ready for action again. No more fooling around risking his life, though. Not for him. No one noticed or paid any heed when he left the bunkhouse at dusk. Just a trip to the outhouse, they would have thought—heavy work and excess food made such trips common. First a little detour to the supply depot, a few sticks of dynamite, then a little action down at the rock.

Loud bangs and roaring blasts downriver masked similar sounds at Bob's rock.

The weather warmed. Four peaceful days passed by. The yard crew, slightly chastised, dumped the logs in more evenly. They floated slowly past Bob without a problem. The foreman, distracted by events further down the river, paid little attention to Bob as long as the logs sailed continually around the oxbow and by Bob's point.

One warm afternoon, after the drive had settled into a routine, with the whole operation running smoothly, the foreman paid Bob a visit. The snow had melted near the riverbank. The foreman found Bob seated on a folded coat, his lunch box open, the warm spring sun hot on his face. The logs floated peacefully past, the current slower now as the freshet had already peaked.

"Hello boss," Bob greeted the foreman pleasantly. "The logs are moving just like you asked."

The foreman stared out at the water,

at the hundreds of logs floating by. His face darkened. "Where's the rock I hired you to watch?"

"Oh that," Bob answered. "Blew that bugger to hell out of there days ago. It was blocking the drive."

"Well, damn," the foreman replied, a devious smile flitting across his face. "Why hell man, you just blew yourself out of a job."

Bob was angry. "No way. You said extra pay if I kept the logs moving. They're moving and I made them move. We shook on it."

"Sorry Bob, old boy. No rock, no job. That may be how they do things down in the Miramichi, but we do things differently here."

9

NEXT IN LINE

The small, one room shop sat perched precariously between the riverbank and the street. It was crowded when I entered. Cecil the barber was working on some good-looking guy, Cecil's snipping scissors making great tufts of dark hair fall on the floor. I found a chair in the corner by the stove to wait my turn.

A large window gave Cecil a clear view of the street and the traffic through town while he cut hair. He could also see Hill Street and view the people visiting the town's new grocery store. A smaller window in the back provided a view of the river. Looking down, we could see the town's famous salmon pool. Today, ninety feet below us, a number of fly fishermen lined up in the rain to try their luck at the early July run.

"Wet day out there," Cecil's young customer said, watching the rain bounce off the pavement.

"Wet days are my busiest," Cecil told him.

"Not too good for haying, though," someone spoke up.

Cecil's young victim admired his new hairdo in the mirror, paid Cecil, said goodbye to everyone, and left. Cecil placed the bill carefully in a drawer. A rugged-looking farmer climbed into Cecil's chair. I glanced quickly around. I was fifth in line.

The farmer settled comfortably into the elevated chair and stretched out his legs. Cecil shook bunches of black hair from a large white cloth and fastened it securely about the farmer's neck.

"How's Walter's new store doing?" the farmer asked.

"Very well it seems," Cecil answered. "The parking lot's always full. People are certainly wheeling cartloads of stuff out of there."

"Didn't take Walter long to build his own store after taking over the business," the farmer observed.

"Oh, he needed a modern place," Cecil said. "It's the only serve yourself store in town. People love to gather up their own stuff, until it's time to pay for it."

"Walter Dyer's a lucky young man," the farmer said. "His Dad really set him up, gave him a great start. Old Ed never had it easy like that. He worked hard. Pulled some fast ones too."

The farmer glanced around to see who was present. When he continued, he spoke with assurance. "Ed started in business as a cattle buyer. It was the only way we had to sell beef back then. I can remember, out in the field, working at the potatoes, I'd see a cattle truck drive out to the pasture. Then Dad and a buyer would walk among the cows. They'd do some tall dickering, and that evening, at milking time, we'd run some of our best animals into the barn. There were a lot of cattle buyers, but Ed was the best. He really enjoyed being ahead of the others."

I spoke up. "What did he do with them all?"

"Oh, most of the animals he bought, the best anyway, were shipped to Montreal. In the fall Ed often shipped a freight car every week. Still, his meat counter was the best around, so he was handling a lot of beef. The farmers were paid good money when they needed it, cash in their pockets when the potatoes were still in the ground."

A frail man with white hair sat in the corner near me. He peered sharply at the farmer in the chair and asked, "Did Collins work for Ed Dyer?"

"Collins." The farmer eyed the speaker.

"You mean red-headed Collins, the guy who drove the big truck. Oh yes, Collins worked with Ed for years. They slaughtered the meat for the store at Collin's farm. Ran a feeder lot there too. After he came back from prison, Collins moved into that shack on Mechanic Street. I think Ed had taken over the farm by then. Walter still keeps a bunch of feeder cattle out there."

The farmer vacated the chair and paid Cecil. "So long," he said.

"See you," someone answered.

The white-haired man took the farmer's place.

I was now fourth in line.

Cecil glanced at the salmon pool while shaking loose hair from the shoulder cloth. "I think someone's hooked a fish," he said.

"It's putting up a fight," someone added.

"Must be a salmon," the white-haired man said. "By the way it's bending that rod."

Cecil draped the cloth around his new customer and picked up the clippers.

"Collins probably sold his farm to Dyer," I offered, attempting to renew the conversation. "He had lots of money when he lived on Mechanic Street, and he didn't seem to have a job."

"I can vouch for that," a new voice in the discussion said.

Looking his way, I recognized a taxi driver, only he seemed much older than I remembered. Then again, it had probably been ten years since I'd last seen him.

"I took Collins to the liquor store every week for over a year. It's over forty miles up there and back, and Collins paid me well. He liked good whiskey, and he dressed well too. He always seemed to have new clothes. The shack wasn't much, but we sure had great times there."

"Why was Collins in prison?" I asked. "I never heard about any trial. Guess I've been away too long."

The man in the chair turned away

from the picture window and looked straight at me. "A great many cattle farmers could tell you that," he said coldly.

He had the floor and our complete attention. We waited quietly.

"Do you want to hear about Collins? I can tell you about Collins. I'm retired and live in town now, but I farmed my whole life out back of the mountain. We never saw a government man during the war years. The country had no time for things like that then. Of course, my farm was rather remote, up the back road there.

"Then one day, it was in forty-seven I'm sure, right in the middle of binding, a new pick-up drove into the yard and a smart-looking, well-dressed fellow got out. He was tall, red-headed, and a real convincing talker. He told us he was a government vet, that he had to test all the cattle, especially for TB. That with the new creamery being built it was mandatory, all cows had to be tested if we wanted to ship cream. He said it was free, so the boys and I quit the oats and rounded up the whole herd for him, all nineteen head. The vet hauled out this kit, needles and syringes and everything, and he proceeded to test them. Well, the four best animals we had, including one big steer, he turned them down for TB. I tell you the boys and I were scared to death. Uncle Bill had just died of TB, and many people we knew were in the sanitorium. I asked the vet, what should we do? Burning them'd be best, he told me bluntly, or at least bury them.

"Lord, I was upset. We hadn't seen any cash since we'd sold the pulp in May. Here it was September and I was supposed to destroy the beef we needed to live on.

"The vet told me he knew how I felt. Said perhaps they could go for fox meat, or pet food, if I could find a buyer. But that we'd have to be careful. If the neighbours found out our farm had TB, they'd insist on the entire place being quarantined. Then we wouldn't even sell potatoes let alone milk or cream.

"The next day didn't a cattle buyer show up. It'd been weeks since we'd seen one. He asked me if we had any cattle for sale. I looked him straight in the eye. Just happen to have four nice head, I told him.

"He bought those beef for close to nothing, just like he knew I had to sell. We never told a single neighbour, just the boys and I knew. It was good to get something for them, but it really bothered me, knowing they'd ship them, TB or not. Well, that vet traveled all over the back country for over two years, and he found hundreds of healthy cattle with TB. The farmers never spread the word. Who wants their neighbours to know your cows have TB? Then the son of a bitch became careless. He started to hit farms closer to town, farms closer together, and people became suspicious.

"The authorities were informed and the police called in. It was all a hoax. The vet turned out to be Collins and he couldn't test anything. He bought hundreds of prime stock for a fraction of their worth and he worked for Dyer."

Listening, I was shocked. The story was new to me, and hard to believe. I glanced around the small shop, at the other listeners. I could see that they'd heard it all before and believed it. "I never heard tell of any trial," I blurted out. "Was Dyer ever charged with anything?"

"I can explain that," the taxi-driver said quietly.

All eyes looked to him. The scissors snipped loudly in the quiet of the shop. Rain drummed softly on the shop's low roof.

"Collins and I became great friends," the taxi driver told us. "I learned plenty on our trips up the river."

"A good thing the liquor store isn't any closer," Cecil interrupted, perhaps hoping to ease the tension.

"Yes sir," the taxi driver agreed. "If we

had an outlet in town the taxis would all go broke."

The old farmer in the chair climbed down, paid Cecil, and left. The taxi-driver took his place. I was now third in line. Cecil shook his white cloth again, making the hair on the floor a little thicker.

The taxi driver stared out into the rain, toward the store, and spoke again. "The day Collins was locked into jail he had a visitor, a lawyer. The farmers are irate, the lawyer told him. You made them look foolish. They'll testify in droves. You can expect ten or twelve years, for sure. I'll make you a deal. Don't implicate anyone else. Tell the judge you were well paid for every cow you handled, that it was all your own idea, and no one else was in on it.

"Then the lawyer added a clincher. He told Collins to plead guilty, spare them a trial, and Ed would continue his salary for every day spent in prison. Collins did as he was told. The judge gave him three years in prison, but he was back home after only two. Most people never knew where he was—thought he was in Alberta, or up on the dew line.

"Collins spent a lot of money, wore nice clothes, and was a real high living guy for someone who never worked. We had great times in that old shack, until his money began to run out. I noticed he was getting upset, and that he didn't go for liquor as often. One day he called me, real moody and down. We drove upriver. He bought some rum. On the way back he had me pull into a gravel pit. We finished the first bottle right there and I'll tell you, yes sir, I heard an earful that day."

Cecil laid down the clippers and picked up a straight razor. Someone said the salmon was still on the line, putting up a fight.

"What did you hear?" I asked.

"Collins said he'd been to see Dyer, and that he told Dyer he was running out of money. Ed wasn't very sympathetic. He laughed at Collins. Told him he spent too much. To come back to work for him. Had some jobs for him. He'd paid what he'd agreed to pay and now the fun was over.

"'No way,' Collins told him. 'The fun's just beginning. Prison wasn't fun, not even a little bit.' He told Ed that he owed him and that he'd better keep on paying.

"Anyhow, Collins asked me to take him to Woodstock, back to see the judge. He'd warned Ed, he told me. Told him that unless he paid up, he'd go to the authorities and tell them everything, all that he should have told them before.

"Well, I couldn't take him the next day, a Tuesday, because I was booked up, but I did drive him down on Thursday, and I took him for free. We talked all the way down. Collins told me that Ed just laughed at him. Laughed and told him to go ahead. So, he damned well did.

"We left town right after lunch, and Collins was in the judge's office for over an hour. Gave him the whole story.

"I bought the rum that day and we found a back road on the way home. We drank to Ed Dyer, to the end of Ed, we said. We bought some lunch about nine, and I dropped Collins off at his shack about ten-thirty. I took him right to the kitchen door, just like the neighbours said. He went inside and closed the door and that was the last time I ever saw him, swear to God."

Cecil unwrapped the white cloth just as the taxi driver finished his story. The taxi driver climbed out of the chair, paid Cecil, and left.

I was now second in line.

"That salmon is putting up some fight," Cecil said, as he put the money away. "They haven't landed it yet."

A man about forty wearing a blue shirt and matching pants climbed into the chair. His outfit suggested he worked at the local Irving garage. We soon learned that he was a volunteer fireman.

"It was a little before eleven when we heard the boom," he recounted. "It blew that shack all to hell. You could hear the explosion all over town. We were there in less than eight minutes but there wasn't much we could do. The windows were blown out. Both doors blown off, the front one lying in the driveway. The flames were shooting through the roof when we drove up in the truck. A neighbour ran toward us, all excited, pointed toward the door and yelled that Collins was inside. A taxi had just brought him home, drunk as a skunk, he told us. The taxi hadn't been gone five minutes before the place blew sky high. We stayed there all night to keep the fire from spreading.

"It was noon the next day before the place cooled down enough to pull Collins out. He was burnt to a crisp—I couldn't even look at him, the thought of it made me sick. I'd never known him that well but knew he liked to party. I'd heard about his trip to prison but never knew why. That taxi driver, though—something phoney about him. Made more money bootlegging than he ever did driving. I used to watch him from the garage, saw him moving the bottles. Now if Collins told everything to the judge, all that about Ed Dyer, why didn't the Mounties check it out? Especially with Collins blown up like that."

A man by the rear window had been sitting quietly, watching the salmon fishermen, listening to everyone ramble on. Now he turned to regard those of us left in the shop.

"Oh, we checked him out, all right," he told us. "I was still in the force back then."

I observed the man's strong build and steel grey hair. A retired Mountie, I figured.

"Collins talked to the judge. I read the report. He was our only witness, and all of a sudden he was gone. There wasn't much evidence. The place had a propane stove. They've been known to explode a time or two. Collins must have walked into the kitchen, too tipsy to notice the fumes, switched on a light or lit a match for a smoke, and boom! He was gone. Ashes don't leave much evidence."

The volunteer fireman interrupted the man. "Something I was curious about at the time. Both doors had been locked. I know because the back one was still in one piece and like I said the other one had been blown onto the driveway. We looked them both over. The neighbours told us that Collins never locked a door in his life. Hardly anybody does in this town. Seemed to me someone didn't want Collins to make it out of that fire alive."

"They needn't have worried," the retired Mountie said. "Collins never had a chance."

The volunteer fireman checked his reflection in the mirror, grinned, paid Cecil, said good-bye, and left. We watched as he crossed the street in the rain. The retired Mountie took his place in the chair.

I was next in line.

Cecil was looking out the window. "Damn," he said. "That salmon got away on him."

"The big ones often do," the retired Mountie said.

10

HAULING POTATOES

John was a little worried coming down Barker's Hill, but everything turned out fine. The sledding was good, the load didn't push the horses too much, and they soon pulled up to the potato warehouse in Bath. There was a long line-up of teams, some hauling huge sleds of thirty or more barrels. While John waited to unload, he talked with other farmers he knew. They asked about his dad.

"How is Joe doing?" they asked. "Not laid up, I hope?"

John explained that his Dad was still

in bed, that it would be another month before he could help with the hauling. "It took a little longer for me," he said. "I used the pulleys, hauled the barrels up half full, then lugged up enough potatoes in baskets to fill them."

"Good man," they told him.

He had lots of help dumping the barrels into the grader when his turn came. They kept him busy placing the empties back on the sled. He was tying them in place when a big, roughly dressed man walked over from the railway station. He seemed familiar to John. The man approached slowly, looking up and down the row of sleds, until he spotted John.

"Are you going up through Danny's Woods on your way home?" he asked.

"Sure will," John answered, observing the man's beard, his heavy coat and worn boots.

It was Matt Sullivan, from over on the hill, not far from John's farm.

"I'm just down from the Tobique,

been working in the woods for six weeks. Came down on the train. Saw the horses over here and thought I might catch a drive. You're Joe's boy, aren't you? I got to get out and see my family."

"Just throw your stuff on the sled there and climb aboard," John told him, thinking it would be fun. Someone to talk to. Stories about the lumber woods, about lumber camps and working on the Tobique. The prospect excited him.

It was not to be.

Sullivan chucked his stuff between two barrels at the back and climbed in after them, disappearing completely out of sight. A bit chagrined, John climbed onto the front. Seated on a barrel he'd turned upside down, he picked up the reins and started the horses back up Barker's hill, toward home. He didn't notice his passenger pull a bottle of rum from his coat, a bottle he'd bought in Perth on his way through, and had already christened.

With his team rested and the sled

much lighter, John made good time. Within forty minutes they'd left the main road and started up through Danny's woods. This quiet shortcut soon brought them within sight of home. It was here the road divided. John lived to the left, while Matt lived on the right, a half-mile up over the hill.

"All right, Matt," John yelled. "Time to get off. Your wife's waiting."

There was no answer. John looked back. There was no sign of Matt, nothing. The horses were restless. John held the reins tightly while he climbed and strained to see where Sullivan was. He found him sleeping. No—John spotted the empty rum bottle—he was unconscious. "The old bugger! That's what he's been doing."

It created a problem. The horses didn't want to take Matt home. No way. They could see their own warm barn, sense their own supper. John considered tying a rope to Matt's feet and hauling the sled from under him. Instead, he swung the team to the right. The horses balked, objected, hesitated, but with encouragement they went, up over the hill to where John could see Matt's old weather-beaten house.

He decided to drop him at the gateway. No, he'd passed out. He had to take him in, to break a trail to the house. A huge drift blocked the driveway. The horses had trouble climbing over it, then more trouble as they struggled to break a trail through the snow toward the house. John noticed Mrs. Sullivan standing in the doorway, two or three ragged urchins crowded around her. She was not happy. Stiff, scowling, legs braced and hands on her hips, she glared at John.

"How dare you bring my man home in a state like that," she yelled.

With her tangled, unkempt hair blowing freely, and wearing a dirty ragged dress to her knees, she stared right at John. "I wait and I wait for Matt to come with some money and you bring him home drunk!"

The woman's words struck John like bullets.

"Get out!" she yelled. "Just dump him and get out."

It wasn't easy. The snow was deep and unpacked. Close to tears, and terribly mortified, young John struggled with the horses, finally got them turned around, pulled Matt off, and then headed home.

It had been a long day for a sixteen-year-old boy. After the horses were watered, fed, and bedded down for the night, John walked slowly toward the house, to his own supper. First though, he took time to visit his Dad, slowly recuperating from appendicitis.

"How could she?" he asked. "I didn't know he was drinking. I never got the old bugger drunk. I worked so hard to get him home."

"Easy, son," his father answered gently. "You'll never get any thanks for bringing a man home in that condition. I remember poor old Uncle Mike. I often took him home after playing for a dance.

I just opened the kitchen door and let him crawl inside. Aunt Kate would scream if she saw me, so I never hung around, scurried out of there as fast as I could. We played for many dances, Mike and me. He was quite good on the fiddle, played really well, but he sometimes got pretty drunk. Poor old Aunt Kate! She always blamed me. It was the people who enjoyed the music, who thought they should treat the fiddler. I was just the kid on the piano.

"Now, Matt's woman! Starved, frustrated, and afraid to face the truth, she had to light into somebody, and you were the only one there."

A hard lesson for a young boy, one John always remembered.

11

A BOTTLE OF RUM

Ambrose drove his pickup into town to buy a few groceries and a bottle of rum. It was on the way home that he came across old Dan. He was standing by the road hoping for a ride. Poor Dan, a bit of a hard luck case, you had to pick him up.

Ambrose knew that as soon as Dan was in the pickup, he'd spot the bottle of rum.

"What's in the bag?" Dan asked.

"Oh, just a bottle of rum I got for my wife," Ambrose told him.

"Good trade," Dan said.

12

BIG MONEY

It's difficult to comprehend the changes in farming over the last seventy-five years.

Our neighbours were buying new tractors. I asked Dad why we didn't buy one.

"We own two nice horses, George and Molly, have plenty of horse-drawn equipment, and work our butts off," he told me. "We grow five acres of potatoes. Except for the fertilizer, it costs us very little. It's our main source of income. We'd need another five acres to pay for a tractor, and still no more income for us.

Then we'd need a truck, a potato warehouse, and special equipment for the tractor. First thing we'd be growing forty acres, same income as now, and where are we going to find forty acres of level land on this old side hill farm?"

So, we were stuck with Molly and George, our faithful horses, for the next while anyhow.

Everyone was busy when haying time came around. The hay was mowed, raked, then forked into bunches. The bunches were carefully turned to dry in the sun. The horses never minded the work—they knew the hay was for their winter feed.

The big day came when we put the rack on the wagon to haul the hay into the barn. We maneuvered the wagon carefully to one side of the barn floor so that we'd have room on the other side to bring a horse out to haul the warp line. My brother set the hay fork into the load and George and I hauled a huge bundle up into the mow. Dad and another brother forked it by hand away back into the mow. The heat in the mow was outrageous. After the wagon was unloaded, we sat outside to drink cold water from our spring. It was the best water ever, and right from our own spring.

My father dipped into the bucket with a dipper, took a long drink, then held up the dipper and said, "Someday we'll pay big money for this."

Little did he know that the price would reach two dollars a bottle, far more than the price of gasoline.

13

I POUNCED

I didn't know the snow was deep.

I just knew I had to go out. I scratched the door

and looked toward my missus.

She smiled and opened the door for me.

The deck was covered with deep snow.

I started to climb up a steep bank to get off.

The snow gave way and down I went.

The snow closed in and there I was, trapped under the deck.

I ran around like crazy.

It was big and dark in there.

Weeks went by. How does a cat tell time?

I was hungry. There was nothing to eat.

Then I heard a sound. I sat quietly, listening,

looking through the shadowy dark.

It was a mouse! I pounced.

My first dinner in forty days!

14

TWO OLD CROWS

Two old crows sat in a tree
      laughing and laughing at you
and at me.
      What have we done, I wanted to
know,
      that two old crows would laugh at
us so.

Whenever we walked it was always
      the same,
      the old crows would start laughing
again.

If you ever find out, please let me know,
why the crows laugh at us so.

15

BUTCH

There is no greater bond than that of a boy and his dog.

Butch the bird dog lived at a time dogs were expected to help with the farm work. Their boys trained them to earn their keep. Butch first saw the Hill farm as a tiny puppy. Brian, the oldest Hill boy, declared that the little pup was an English setter, and avowed that someday it would be a great bird dog.

Butch grew very fast. His finely shaped head, long floppy ears, and friendly demeanour endeared him to the entire family. Though his colour scheme seemed to be Holstein—all black and white blotches—his thick chest and muscular build were more like a beef variety; a bit of Hereford perhaps.

Regardless of colour, Butch was all dog. He could run, bark, point, jump through a hoop, and grab a biscuit in mid-air, just like a real genuine dog. In fact, no doubt about it, Butch fast became Brian's pride and joy. An exciting, highly trained champion bird dog. The absence of an official pedigree didn't matter. Brian insisted that love, tender care, and expert training were all that really counted.

A natural part of that expertise was gun training. No, not target shooting: noise tolerance. Starting the first summer, when Butch was three months old, Brian used cap guns, paper bags and twenty-twos, with a promise of shotguns the following summer.

Early in June, shortly after little Butch's arrival, Mrs. Hill began her annual house cleaning. A tireless woman, with her hair tightly tied in a bandanna and a long skirt to protect her knees, she started upstairs and began to work her way down, subjecting the bedrooms, living room, kitchen, and even the pantry to her mop and rags. Her cleaning that year penetrated into dark recesses that hadn't seen a broom in ages. In the pantry, behind the flour barrel, she found a mysterious, unopened can. Dented, rusted, and its paper covering long gone, it appeared to have fallen there years before. She picked it up and moved it to the porch. Later, she asked Brian if he wouldn't mind taking a few minutes out of training his favourite dog to take the can to the farm dump.

"Sure thing, Mom," Brian told her, cap gun in hand. "Next time I go out." And promptly forgot about it.

As the short, cool days of fall neared, Butch the bird dog increased in weight, speed, and knowledge. He established his favourite sleeping quarters under the kitchen stairs, the steep narrow stairs the

Hill children climbed reluctantly when ordered up the "wooden hill" instead of the fancy front room stairs used only on special occasions. Here, snuggled among wet boots and stray jackets, Butch had his own private cave. A heavy wooden box, used for storing stove wood, separated Butch from the kitchen stove. It was nice and warm. Butch felt very safe in his cozy nook, out of heavy traffic, his tail safe from careless boot treads.

The snow came, the storms blew, the snow melted, and soon it was spring again. Mrs. Hill started to feel a strong urge to clean house once more. The scrubbing, shining and dusting progressed with increasing speed from bedrooms to living room, kitchen to pantry, even managing to reach the porch this time. And it was there that Mrs. Hill found the can, slightly more rusted than before, sitting exactly where she had left it one year earlier.

Frustrated but understanding, Mrs. Hill dropped the unopened can into the blazing fire of the kitchen stove. She walked quietly back to the porch, scrub pail in hand, reflecting that Brian must have been so busy training Butch that he hadn't remembered to take the rusty can to the dump. Meanwhile, Butch, all curled up safe and secure under the stairs, enjoyed pleasant dreams of chasing squirrels and rabbits.

The soup in the can, for such it was, gurgled, bubbled, steamed and strained against its confinement before finally exploding violently like a miniature bomb.

Harrumph, boom, thump!

Covers, lifters, pots, ashes, blazing cinders, great clouds of soot, and a generous supply of peas were driven upward and outward, undoing in seconds whole weeks of cleaning and dusting. Protected by the wood box from the initial blast, but terrified by the tremendous din, Butch flew upward and outward, straight into the storage box, strewing sticks of wood across the kitchen floor. Propelled by pure terror, he shot straight out of the kitchen like a torpedo, leaving the neatest big round hole in the screen door behind him.

Yes sir, it sure is interesting how one second can erase months of careful training.

Butch never graduated to shotguns. A cap gun was sufficient to put him through two doors. Although he did go back to sleeping in his cozy nook under the back stairs, the family was careful to lay their boots down gently when they pulled them off at night, and to dump the wood for the stove in the storage box ever so carefully.

16

BURNT HILL BROOK

Timothy was buttering a piece of toast when he heard the Model A come up the driveway. He rushed to the window, toast in hand, just in time to see Archie pull up outside.

"There's Archie now," he yelled excitedly. "He said he'd be here early."

"Better finish your breakfast, Timothy," his mother advised. "Could be a long day."

Timothy stuffed the toast into his mouth while watching his older brother, John, load the fishing poles into the rumble seat.

"They'll wait for you," his mother assured him.

Timothy didn't take any chances. He finished eating while standing over his plate. Grabbing his old farm cap, he stepped out.

"Still keen to go are you, Timothy?" Archie asked with a grin.

"You bet!"

"Don't forget the lunch," Timothy's mother called from the doorway.

"Don't worry," John assured her. "We have everything."

"I'll take care of them," Archie called, as the Model A puttered to life. "We'll be back tomorrow night."

Archie was short and stocky and possessed a jaunty air accentuated by his bright red hair, which he wore in a flat brush cut. Timothy was really taken with Archie's new jeans and fancy work boots, in contrast to his own bib overalls and cheap farm boots. John was not so easily impressed. The tallest of the three, he usually wore his school dress pants, but on this day had downgraded to work pants. Still, he had to hand it to Archie, who at only twenty years of age owned a car, worked in a sawmill, and had a reputation as a skilled hunter and woodsman.

Timothy squeezed into the middle of the Model A between John and Archie, the gear shift between his knees. John sat next to the door, with Archie behind the wheel. The tiny Ford started down the dirt road. Timothy could hardly contain his excitement as they turned onto the Juniper Road. He remembered Archie inviting him along, how quickly he'd said yes. Archie often came to the farm to play music with John. They frequently planned fishing trips that didn't include Timothy. Now, thirteen years old and accepted at last, Timothy looked proudly from Archie to John as the Ford stirred up spirals of dust behind them.

"Did you bring the stuff for Charlie?" John asked.

"Yes sir. Right in the back," Archie

answered. "Charlie'll be happy to see us after six weeks. We have tobacco, tea, sugar, even a bottle of rum."

"Why would anyone take a job like that?" Timothy asked.

No one offered an answer as Archie shifted into second gear. The Model A climbed a long hill that twisted between small fields. One farmer, with faith in the weather, was mowing a hay field. His team of large black work horses, fresh and eager in the early morning, stepped quickly along.

"They'll soon knock that field down," John said, admiring the spirited team.

"It's a heavy crop, too," Archie added.

When the road levelled out, Archie reached for the gear shift, playfully knocking Timothy on the knee as he shifted into high gear.

Timothy spotted a large steer in one of the fields they passed. "A lot of meat on that animal."

"Yes sir, big steaks on that fellow," Archie agreed.

A poorly mowed field drew a critical comment. "They cut that on the shares," John stated.

"I think the field got the biggest share," Archie laughed.

Soon they were traveling through a wooded area. With no farms or farm animals to comment on, the conversation turned back to Charlie. Timothy remembered Charlie quite well from his occasional stops by the farm. The sight of the bearded, dirty, unkempt creature shuffling up the driveway was welcome. It added variety to a lonely farm existence.

Wanting to help the poor fellow out, their dad faithfully gave Charlie a couple of days work each time he visited. He seldom earned his pay. What little wood he cut, or hay he raked, never merited his wages. Still, Dad would look for jobs Charlie could do, always outdoors, as they didn't want him in the house. Charlie never sang, played cards, or told stories, and he always smelt bad. He was considered quite boring. Far more interesting were the stories that constantly circulated about him.

"I hear you pulled some great pranks on Charlie when he lived over in Tarrytown," John said to Archie.

"It was all in fun," Archie responded. "If Charlie would wash and change his clothes now and then, maybe he wouldn't be tormented so much."

"He does smell a little bad," Timothy admitted.

Archie steered around a huge pothole. "I think we had him a little panicky one night. Someone tied the door of his shack shut while I put a pail over the stove pipe. There was smoke coming out of cracks in that shack everywhere!"

Timothy laughed. "He should have a back door!"

"It was the barber who really got Charlie stirred up," Archie said seriously. "Someone in the shop asked how to find a bootlegger. Cecil told him how to get to Charlie's shack. I was still there when the guy came back. 'You sent me to a crazy man,' he yelled at Cecil. 'You damned son of a bitch.' Everyone in the place laughed. They knew that the barber sent all the strangers up to Tarrytown to pester Charlie. This guy thought he really was at a bootleggers. He figgered the old lad wouldn't sell him anything cuz he thought he was a cop. There he was half-pissed and telling Charlie over and over again that he wasn't a cop and Charlie getting madder and madder."

As they approached the Miramichi River, the road dipped down into the town of Juniper. Timothy gawked open-eyed at the great yards of logs and all the newly sawed boards neatly stacked around the mill. The older boys laughed. They knew Timothy had never been that far from home before.

They were soon through the settlement. A small bridge allowed passage over the river, and before long they were on a company logging road. A small sign warned drivers to be aware of logging trucks. The trail was narrow, smoothed out somewhat by a bulldozer, but full of potholes and huge mud puddles, often a foot deep. Archie deftly slipped into low gear and crawled through them.

John picked up the conversation. "So, Charlie felt a little pestered when all those drunks came around to bother him. Cecil must have enjoyed that."

"That was when McGinley gave Charlie a job at the Burnt Hill camp," Archie said. "Charlie was the handyman, cut firewood for the cook, helped feed and care for the horses. I heard he even filed saws."

"Yes, I heard he became good at filing," John commented.

"I wonder if he washed and smelt any better," Timothy felt obliged to add.

"It was so cold at camp nobody would notice," Archie explained.

The trail gradually climbed higher, rougher, and rockier, permitting a better view of the surrounding hills, all heavily forested, and each a darker colour depending on the distance.

Archie told Timothy how Charlie wouldn't go back to town after the log drive ended, that he wanted to stay at the camp where people wouldn't bother him. McGinley, the contractor, let him stay. He could look after the surplus supplies, keep porcupines from chewing the place down, and chase groundhogs out of the hay and oats. He could also make some repairs in his spare time. McGinley promised someone would check on him over the summer. That was Archie's job, to bring Charlie supplies, after which he could do some real fishing at Burnt Hill Brook.

"Hey, look at that," Timothy shouted as a big buck deer jumped clear of the road and bounded into the trees.

They crested the hill and started to go downhill. The woods began to close in on them. Alders soon threatened to block the way, and Archie expressed fear that they would scratch his car. Gradually the strong-smelling alders gave way to spruce, fir, and cedar, and the road smoothed out. Archie halted the car at the edge of a narrow, impassable creek, the remnants of a rough log bridge scattered along both banks.

"We walk from here," Archie said with a grin.

"What's the time?" John asked.

Archie checked his pocket ben. "Ten to twelve."

"Do we eat here, or after we cross?" Timothy asked.

"Might as well wade over and eat while our feet dry," Archie suggested.

They ate lunch seated on the far bank, a small fire burning nearby to keep away the flies. Timothy, munching happily on a bologna sandwich, his bare feet resting on a flat rock near the water, marvelled at his good fortune.

"You're getting pretty good on the piano, Timothy," Archie commented between bites of his sandwich. "What do you think, John?"

"Better continue your lessons though. It'd be nice if one of us could read music," John lamented.

"Lessons!" Archie scoffed. "Don't get too good, Timothy, or no one'll listen to you."

"I'd be pretty long-haired then, wouldn't I?" Timothy laughed.

Inevitably the talk returned to Charlie, to the camp, and to the great fishing they expected to find at Burnt Hill Brook.

"I wonder how Charlie's enjoying the heat," John said. "He must be melting in this hot sun."

"All that underwear keeps him cool," Timothy suggested.

"We'd better get going, it's a long way yet, and we have to walk the whole way," Archie said.

The trail from that point was only a path, a tote road intended for winter sledding. They walked in single file, Archie in front, John next, with Timothy gamely bringing up the rear.

"Do either of you know why Charlie can't stand old Bob?" Archie asked.

"Charlie hates Bob," Timothy said. "He's scared to death of him."

"How do you know?" Archie asked. "What did Bob ever do that was worse than anyone else ever did?"

John took up the story as they plodded slowly along. "Dad asked Charlie if he'd like to help us thresh. We knew he wouldn't care to be in the mow, because that was hard work. Still, Charlie needed the work, so he said he'd be there. The threshing had already started. Bob was feeding the machine, just stuffing the sheaves into it, when Dad saw Charlie coming around the end of the barn. Then he disappeared, gone, and we never saw him again for three weeks.

"He came by one day and Dad asked him if the work had scared him off. 'Well, I came here to work, and I was going to work, until I saw that mad-man you had there,' Charlie told Dad. 'You don't get me anywhere near that fellow. He shot at me once, scared the hell out of me, and ruined my good boots.' He never said much more, thought we didn't believe him.

"So next time Bob came around Dad wasn't long asking him. Well, Bob was a little ashamed, sorry that it happened. 'It was up on the Gulquac,' Bob told Dad. He and Charlie worked at the same camp. One Sunday afternoon the camp was quiet and Bob wandered into the bunkhouse. There was Charlie sound asleep on a bunk away down at the other end, and he had a pair of those expensive high-top rubber boots hung by a lace about three feet over his head. There was Charlie snoring away, all alone in the room, and Bob couldn't resist it. He planned to shoot the laces in two, have the boots fall on Charlie's nose and scare the hell out of him. I guess his aim was a bit low. He hit the toe of one boot and tore the whole bottom out of it. They fell down all right, right on Charlie's face, and

Charlie pretty near went through the roof."

"Oh, my lord," Archie said, astounded. "I never heard about that. Bob's '38 would have sounded like dynamite in a room like that. Must have scared the piss out of the poor guy."

Timothy was amused at the expression. "Do people really get that scared?"

"Bob was kind of sorry about it," John added. "We never spread it around much."

"We should pull some trick on Charlie," Timothy suggested. "He hasn't seen anyone in weeks."

They turned a bend, broke into a clearing, and there it was. The sight of the camp did not inspire awe, consisting as it did of stumps, weeds, and crumbling shacks. As they drew closer, they identified the horse stables by their large doors and huge manure piles. Archie said the long narrow building with the rough door and two small windows was a bunkhouse. The roof and all four exterior walls were covered with tar paper held on by narrow wooden slats.

Compared to the dark trail the sun in the small clearing seemed excessively bright. The hum of bees and buzzing of flies filled the air. They saw a wide deep stream flowing noisily not far from the stables. A cleared area had left a harsh scar on the near bank, a testament to the large number of logs that had been piled there from the spring drive. Scattered bits of bark and high weeds were all that was left.

The three looked around carefully, especially for wildlife. Deer and bears often lurked in cleared areas where low bushes and grass provided food. They wondered what Charlie was up to, which building he was in. Two squirrels ran down one tree, over the road, and scampered up another. A crow cawed loudly from a high branch.

John led the way toward the long, paper-covered bunkhouse. His two companions close behind, all stooping low, they edged up to the nearest small window. The four tiny panes of glass were black and dusty, the interior of the bunkhouse dark. John and Archie peered inside, sighting along the length of the bunks, shading their eyes with their hands, their noses close to the glass. Timothy hung back as there was no room for him.

"I see him," John whispered. "There, in the last bunk."

"That's him all right, and he's sound asleep," Archie said.

Archie turned to Timothy, clasped his arm lightly, and led him toward the door.

"Quietly now," he instructed. "You creep in and wake Charlie up. You said you wanted to surprise him. Grab his beard. He'll think a bear's got him."

Archie slipped quickly back to the window to see the fun.

Timothy pushed the door slightly inward. A smell of hot stale air wafted out past him. He started to feel less keen about the venture. He looked toward the others, who waved him on. Timothy knew that he was caught. He had to go on. Opening the door a little wider, he stepped inside. He held his breath, let his eyes adjust to the gloom, and began creeping forward.

He could see the old man easily now. So too the grinning faces in the window. Charlie was lying in the second bunk from the end, one leg hanging over the edge, a heavy boot on the floor. His head and shoulders were propped up by some folded blankets. One jacket clad arm lay across his chest, the other extended toward the floor. The sleeping figure's face was completely masked by his bushy hair and straggly beard which hung down over his jacket front.

Gathering his nerve, Timothy stepped quickly forward, reached out, felt the greasy hair in his fingers, and gave a slight pull. With little effort the whole face came free in his hand. Bare teeth flashed in the murky gloom. The stench of death filled the air, the force of it wrenching Timothy backwards. Lurching toward the door, he dropped the sickening burden and retched the contents of his stomach. The room spun and went dark as he collapsed on the floor.

He awakened to the sound of a gurgling brook, water slapping against rocks. Two anxious faces peered over him.

"I guess he's all right," he heard Archie say.

"Seems Charlie wanted to surprise us," John murmured.

Timothy climbed slowly to his feet, wondering at the wetness in the front of his overalls. Understanding came, and he was embarrassed.

Archie sat down on an old log. "I'm going right back to Juniper," he said. "We can't leave Charlie like that one minute longer than we have to."

"I can't walk back tonight," Timothy groaned.

"That's all right, Timothy. You and John will stay here while I get help."

"You should eat first," John suggested. "We still have sandwiches."

"Sure, it's early yet," Archie agreed. "Let's catch some fish too."

The call-to-action pushed aside the last remnants of horror. Soon two dozen trout were cooking in a large frying pan borrowed from the cook shack. Burnt Hill Brook had lived up to expectations. Well-fed and rested, Archie departed, promising to be back early the next morning.

John and Timothy set up sleeping quarters near a small fire by the stream. They knew the black flies were bad, but nothing could compel them into one of the buildings. They laid Archie's blanket over some soft boughs and curled up close together under their own.

"That Archie sure is tough, walking back in there alone," John remarked. "The morning would have been fine, really."

"Will he make it, do you think?" Timothy asked, a little worried.

"Sure he will," John reassured him.

Archie was back at the logging camp by noon along with four men from Juniper. The frying pan was soon heaped with trout, enough to make a feast for everyone.

"I guess old Charlie scared the daylights out of you, eh Timothy?" one of the Juniper men teased.

"I thought he was only sleeping," Timothy admitted.

The men removed the body. The boys didn't watch. They sat by the brook instead. Afterward they followed the men down the trail but made no effort to keep them in sight. They talked about the trees, about deer and bears, birds, squirrels and chipmunks, and discussed Archie's new band and Timothy's music lessons, but not once did they mention Charlie.

17

THE NOISE

Something disturbed my sleep. I turned restlessly. My brother Ambrose snuggled up closely looking for warmth. I didn't mind because I knew his sleeping bag was inadequate for the cold. Suddenly I was awake, or was I dreaming I was awake? That strange chewing sound, what was it? I could hear the river turning and the splashing of the waterfall, but that odd noise, what could it be?

Ambrose woke up. "What's out there?"

I crawled toward the tent flap,

unzipped the door, and peeked out. The night was still dark, but I could see a black shape in the water. It was big and moved swiftly, oblivious to our tent only twenty feet away. I looked closer. It was a huge black bear. It leaped toward the falls, drove its nose into the water, and emerged with a large trout in its mouth.

"It's only a big bear eating its breakfast," I told Ambrose. "Go back to sleep."

18

LETTER FROM BILL

S*ept 1956*

D ear Tom,
Hark to the voice of one crying in the wilderness, then picture to yourself the unlovely spectacle of a big cussed, unmitigated two-fisted rugged sour long haired pussy-faced, insignificant, infernal etc. etc. etc. man like me writing a letter. Haw, haw, haw.

Well, I don't reckon there is much news to tell you, Tom ol' Buck, except what's goin' on round the turkey ranch here. It's been rainin' most of the day. What part of the day wasn't rainin', we spent working on the digger. Reckon we might dig potatoes tomorrow if it ain't rainin'. Haw, haw, haw.

Frank Toner, the half-breed son of a greaser, was just hyar. He had the woman and Bill Frennan's kids. He got one of the pups. I bet he will put a Grand Falls branding iron on its rump. The white livered card shark. I figured he was giving us the double cross. Tim, I've shore felt in my bones that I'm the boy slated to brand that big bull, stealin' my dog. The hog wallapin' snooper. I'll ring his neck yet, by God, you bet your life.

The cost of liven has shore gone up. Look at the price of eggs compared to the wear and tear on a hen's ass. Awful, ain't it? We wuz picken spuds fer J. B. the first of last week. We got somewhere 'round 200 barrels. He threshed our grain one afternoon the week yuh left. We hafta pick 300 barrels tuh pay the ornery brute.

We got 'round 400 bushels of oats though for our bother.

Brains dug J.B's Katahdins for him, $10 per day. Albert Hall got $8 per day.

Amby and I manufactured a fence across the big flat last Friday. We tore the one down by the machine shed and built one straight across from the corner of the one at the potato field tearing part of it down. We purchased a plough at Ed Martins junkyard for $8. It's almost the spitting image of the one Brains had. Brains took his home last summer. It's a dead bet he's playen his own game… oh I am out of breath… and I am out of names to call him. If I talked forever… I'd never be able to do him justice. But me a gun for a minute.

W.M. Rideout was home for the weekend. Amby and I were down yesterday. He took the 303 along but Arch left, so we talked to Jack awhile and came home. W.M. was packing up to hitchhike back around five o'clock. The honourable R. Tucker was in one night the week you left. He didn't stay for the night. The same night Archie brought him in, Amby and Arch went to Indian Point for a music practice.

Mr. R and Tucker have gone away the hell out over the hill fifteen miles or so and built a camp to hunt stag. I hope Prince John hangs them both. John Doctor already disarmed Rob of his pea shooters. Remember last spring the mountie took them. Doc John L. phoned him.

I went to two shows last week. And was up to John Cronans one night and played cards. Both shows were westerns and fairly good. Ambrose didn't bother to take Marie on Saturday night but he picked Terrance K. up in town and we went in. It starred Forrest Tucker in "The Quiet Gun." Mother and family and Marie McLeod went down Wed and saw "The Lonely Man." We hauled manure from the calf pen the day or so after you left. Tony was up one day and spun a lot of yarns.

He's getting pretty sick of Joe's gab and of his hogs. He's going to take a course in engineering at or from Francis Xavier. So is Terrence Kilfoil. They both leave this week by Juniper. Tony calculates that it costs more than it's worth but thinks he hasn't much choice. I guess Vince is going away too, back to S.T.C I guess.

Arche just drove in. Amby got out of bed and went out to the back field with him. They are going to shine the car lights around a bit. I expect to hear a gun roar any time now. They took the 8 mm Mauser.

Well, the men never got any venison last night. I've just received orders to get the team harnessed and put to work. Amby said that he would finish the milking. It's eight thirty now. He milked a couple cows. The damn critters want to stay out in the big flat all the time.

Well, I suppose I'd better finish this and go do something, plough that is.

Eva was up Sunday and wanted to get

two books from you. They are "General Science of the Seasons" and "Managing the Classroom." Well, so long. Be seeing you some time. Don't break your neck on the road.

Yours Sincerely,
Bill

19

THE HITCHHIKER

After three weeks of picking potatoes it was time to go home. The farmer drove us across the border and dropped us off at the Perth bridge. Bill and I thanked him, said it was a good place to hitch a ride, and waved goodbye. The cars moved slowly on the bridge. There was lots of room to pull over, and we were ready to hop in.

We waited for over an hour, car after car going by, then finally a big Ford picked us up. The driver, a young man in his twenties, admitted to being tired. He said he'd left London the day before and had driven all night. He was headed for PEI. He looked at me, a boy of eighteen and a total stranger, and asked if I had a driver's license. When I told him I did, he offered me the wheel, jumped into the back seat, and was asleep in minutes.

There we were, my brother and I, driving a nice big car, and an open road. I just wanted to go home to Sussex. It was a good five hour's drive from Perth to Sussex in 1965. We had to drive through the main street of every little town and hamlet, while crossing the Saint John River twice. There was a big new bridge at Hartland, so we never went through the old covered bridge. We were a bit shy of driving through Fredericton, but it wasn't a problem.

When we reached Sussex, the owner was still asleep, so we parked near a sign that pointed out the road to Moncton, put a ten-dollar bill under his horn, gathered our bags, and headed home. A short way down the street, we heard the car start up. We looked back, and the three of us waved to one another as he left.

20

THE BACK RYDERS

The house was quiet when they drove into the yard, with only a dog to greet them. It was a little disconcerting after two days on the road, not having any people around to meet them. The big dog came forward, wagging his tail.

"Hi Butch," said Tim, when he got out. "Say hello to Marie, big fellow."

"It's six o'clock, Tim. Everyone's at supper," Marie suggested.

Tim looked around at the barns and the other buildings. Nothing had changed. There were a couple of extra cars, so there had to be visitors. A sudden yell broke the quiet. They had been spotted.

"Well, look who's here," Tim called, holding out his arms to greet his younger sister Rosalie.

They discovered the rest of the family inside the kitchen of the old farmhouse, finishing their dinner. Places were soon provided for them at the table, making them feel right at home.

Tim hadn't seen much of a future around the farm when he'd graduated from high school the previous summer, and so had left for Oshawa, to work in the auto plant there. Everything had gone well for him. He was young, used to hard work, and quick to learn. Marie had worked in the office, and they'd met while having lunch in the cafeteria. She had had all winter to show Tim her city ways and have him meet her family. When Tim asked her to come to his sister's wedding in July, she'd hesitated.

Her father said, "To Bath, New Brunswick, a two-day trip."

"We could stay one night in Montreal, at my sister's," Marie suggested.

"Better than a motel," Tim laughed.

It was only Wednesday, the wedding not until Friday, but the festivities had already begun. Marie was impressed by how quickly the family had accepted her. They could tell how much Tim loved her.

The yard was soon filled with cars. Tim introduced Marie to the bride and groom. An older sister arrived from Ottawa, with a husband and three kids in tow. The music started, and it seemed everyone had a turn at the piano, fiddles, or guitar. The dancing, singing and playing went on for hours. Finally, around one in the morning, as they retreated out under the stars, Marie pulled Tim toward her, her arms tightly around him. "You never told me your family could play like that. When are you going to perform?"

"The others stole all the talent," Tim joked.

They rose early the next morning. Marie tried to milk her first cow. All her clumsy efforts were in vain. The docile cow gave her a puzzled look.

"I'll show you," Tim volunteered.

He took the pail, sat on the stool, and squirted vigorously for a short while. It soon slowed to a crawl. "Milking was never this hard. I must have milked the easy ones," he admitted.

"Aren't they all the same?" Marie asked.

"Not really," Tim said, giving her a hug.

While others finished the milking, Tim gave Marie a tour of the farm. They walked through the back pasture. It was a new world to her. When she spotted the calves frolicking about, tearing off with their tails held high, she laughed and stopped on a knoll to stare at them.

On the way back to the house, Tim

detoured through a narrow wood that brought them out to a weedy field bordering the highway. In the center of the rough overgrown clearing were lines of heavy stones laid out in a rectangular shape, almost buried in burdocks. Separated from the huge stones by a patch of wild rose bushes and tall unkempt grass, they found the remnants of a small building with two doors and a slanted roof. Tim looked pensively about.

"What's this?" Marie asked.

"That was our two-holer," Tim answered, surveying the collapsed structure.

Marie glanced at the farmhouse on the hill. "A little far to go for a toilet."

"Oh, this was for our country school. We had an outdoor back at the house. The girls used one door and the boys the other. The school was built on those rocks. There was no cellar and the place got a bit cold in the winter. It sat here empty after the buses came, until some farmer hauled it away. It's a potato house now."

"Did you learn anything here?" Marie asked.

"Sure, I did. Learned to read and bother the girls. Come on, I'll show you where I sat."

Tim waded through the burdocks and climbed onto a flat rock, which had once supported a sill. He reached for Marie's hand and helped her up beside him. "Old Clarence had his throne over on that rock, the son of a bitch, and cute little Betty sat over here, in front of me."

"Did you actually have eight grades?" Marie asked, trying to visualize the old school.

"Oh yes, and three or four kids in each. The Women's Institute donated books. They put a library in that corner. I had them all read by Grade 6. Old Clarence played the fiddle, then Mary had us doing pageants, but I liked John. He had us spend all our time skiing, except for the time we spent up in the attic playing in the dark. That was fun, real creepy, until Hilda stepped between the rafters and fell through the ceiling."

"Sure she did." Marie was skeptical.

"Well, one foot went through, and we looked at the hole all winter."

Tim looked fondly at Marie, at her light brown hair and slim, jean-clad figure, and then at the ruins, his mind conjuring up all the ghosts of his youth. Was he ever lucky to have gotten away from there. That long walk into Bath, into the high school, had been more than worth it.

Back at the house, Tim and Marie found the wedding preparations in full swing. Everyone, it seemed, had a job to do.

"Would you and Marie like to pick some raspberries?" Tim's mother asked.

"Do you have cultivated berries now?" Tim wanted to know.

"Up on the mountain the berries are as good as cultivated," Tim's sister Rosalie said.

"You mean up on Carrol Mountain? What about the bears? And if they don't get us, the back Ryders will."

"Don't worry," Rosalie answered. "The bears won't hurt you, and the Ryders left years ago."

"It sounds like those hillbillies you once told me about," Marie said. "Do we need a gun?"

"No, I'll just take you," Tim said. "We'll be safe, especially with all that self-defence stuff you learned in Toronto."

"The Ryders moved to Tarrytown, thank heavens," Tim's mother explained. "And Ted joined the army. Your Uncle Mike said there were lots of raspberries where his crew cut the pulp and logs."

After lunch they headed out, dressed in borrowed jeans and thick shirts for protection against the flies and bushes.

"Try to pick enough for a dozen pies," Rosalie had instructed them. "We have a wedding crowd to feed."

"So, we're finally going to see the top

of the mountain you've talked about so often," Marie said, as they climbed into the red Dodge.

The road was narrow and steep, but passable. Tim had to alternate between low and second gear. They saw two abandoned houses with sagging porches and broken windows. There were small, neglected, side hill fields and lots of thick forest. They kept a close watch for logging trucks that might come barreling down the steep hill toward them.

Beyond the crest, with the trail winding down toward the creek, they found the cuttings and the berries. A log road of mud, grass, deep ruts and brush led off to the left. It did not appear to have been used recently, so Tim drove in just far enough to clear the main road. The hot July sun and strong, pungent odour of dead wood greeted them as they climbed out of the Dodge. Stretched out on both sides for acres were low stumps interspersed with dead branches, covered with rust coloured needles. A few grey stubs and the occasional derelict tree, alive but useless, stood sentinel over the waste. Then there were the raspberries, tall bushes heavy with fruit that grew in abundance everywhere they looked.

"Wow, have you ever seen so many berries?" Tim called to Marie.

Marie came around the car to Tim's side. She was less enthusiastic. "Quiet," she whispered, clinging to his arm. "It's so desolate and spooky here. You said there were bears, and who were those people you talked about?"

"Oh, it's beautiful here, Marie." Tim gave her a rough hug. "Just breathe in that rich air and listen to those crickets. The trees are gone but look at all the birds." Holding Marie at arm's length, he inspected her rough, borrowed clothes and laughed. "We have the place to ourselves, just you and me and the squirrels. No one's been here for days. The Ryders are gone. They left years ago."

They started picking where the bushes hung out over the road. The berries were so thick they could grab big handfuls at a time, but they were small, and the pails slow to fill. There was little breeze in the protected clearing and Tim and Marie soon felt the hot sun beating down on them. Gradually the black flies found them.

"How do people get themselves into situations like this?" Marie complained, swatting a fly, leaving a streak of red on her cheek.

"It's not easy," Tim said.

"I only hope the hungry appreciate the pain we're enduring," Marie laughed.

"How many berries does it take to make a dozen pies?" Tim asked. "Should be enough here if the flies don't get us first!"

"Oh, about six million if you just pick the big ones," Marie responded, bouncing a whopper off the back of Tim's head.

They soon forgot the heat and

discomfort in the pleasure of their own company and the blissful seclusion of the wood. A flock of blue jays swooped down to entertain them. Not to be outdone, a woodpecker provided percussion on a dead stub.

Marie waded into some tall bushes searching for larger berries. The crack of a heavy boot on a dry branch caught both her and Tim by surprise. Tim turned to see two men approaching his car. The nearer of the intruders, a heavyset man wearing army boots and khaki pants, carried an old, battered shotgun. A dirty baseball cap with McCains on the front sat tightly on his head, the brim set straight ahead. The second man appeared stunted compared to the first. He wore a pair of battered sneakers and ripped jeans. A wide-brimmed, sweat-stained hat covered his head. Both men wore thick, long-sleeved shirts—to ward off the flies, Tim suspected.

The larger of the two men leaned against the hood of the Dodge, placed the butt of the shotgun against the ground, and stared hard at Tim. "Ain't you Timothy Doyle? Well, we sure ain't seen you in a long while. Gettin' some berries, I see."

"Hello, Ted. It's been a while. I heard you left the country."

The runt leaned against the front fender. He carried a fishing pole and had a plastic fishing basket slung over one shoulder.

"Hello, Herb," Tim addressed him. "You two must be on vacation."

"Always on vacation when you don't have a job." Ted sounded sullen.

"I noticed your McCains cap," Tim said.

"Oh, that." Ted removed the cap to stare at the name. "We picked some rocks for them last spring and I stole the damn thing. I wondered what it said."

Tim took off the soiled cap he'd picked up back at the farmhouse. "Mine has Irving but yours says McCains. You never did get to school much, did you Ted?"

"Enough to scare the shit out of you, if I remember right."

Tim returned Ted Ryder's intimidating stare. He was determined to show no fear today. Why should he? Perhaps the Ryders had changed. Maybe they'd matured since leaving the back of Carrol Mountain. Why the sweat, then? It must be the sun. Yes, the sun and the heat. He knew he was heavier than Ted now, if that meant anything. He remembered back at the old school—how Ted, three years older, had scared him silly. The difference in age meant very little now. Still, he couldn't shake his uneasiness. The Ryders loved to fight and intimidate others. Friendly, Tim knew, until they sized things up.

"Who's that hiding in the bushes back there?" Ted asked casually.

"That's my sister," Tim answered carefully. "She's keen to fill her pail, wants a pie for supper."

A faint smile crossed Ted's face. Herb shied back a ways, as though sensing trouble. Slowly, Ted stood away from the car, leaning forward on the shotgun, which he held by the barrel. He pushed the butt into the soft ground. "Who said you could pick these berries? You Doyles don't own everything, you know."

Tim stared coldly into the menacing face, the probing bitter eyes. The bully thought he could still scare him. A cold shiver threatened to shake Tim's resolve. The least sign of weakness and that bastard would pound on him, just to be mean. And Marie, what would he do to Marie, back in these lonely woods? Bullies prey on weakness, Tim knew, but really they're yellow. Still, there seemed to be no lack of confidence in the armed man's sneering face.

With a snapping of bushes, Marie climbed out onto the road, her pail almost full of fresh red berries. She gave the two Ryders a pleasant smile. "We can make plenty of pies with these,

Tim." Addressing the Ryders, she added, "It's great picking, boys. We have some extra containers. You should pick some."

"No way, not in this heat. I don't even like 'em." Ted gave Marie a sour look. "You want some, Herb?"

Herb shook his head slowly, his heavy hat bobbing up and down. He stared closely at Marie. "You ain't a Doyle," he said in a low voice.

Tim felt a sinking feeling in his gut.

Ted looked from Marie to Tim. His face lit up in triumph. "Why, you're old Tim's lady friend! You need a real man, not that sad excuse. We scared the piss out of Tim years ago, away back at the old school, and look, he's still shaking."

Laughing loudly at his own joke, Ted stomped about on the rough road. He swung the shotgun about like a cane, grabbing the barrel in his huge right hand, and kicked a boot into the soft dirt.

Tim realized he was still carrying his half-filled pail. To hide his agitation, he walked toward the back of the car and opened the trunk. He set the pail inside, then took Marie's pail and set it inside too.

"Is this your car?" Ted asked.

"It will be, after I pay the bank. What's it to you?"

"How could you buy a machine like this?" Ted's voice rose in pitch. "You don't have that kind of money. No way! Your old man bought it."

"My Dad doesn't have any money," Tim said. "Never did. I went to school. Learned to read, and I have a job."

Ted wasn't impressed. "You learned to cheat, that's all. The stupid teachers never looked at us. We were the dirty Ryders from back of the mountain. Stay away from those dirty back Ryders, your Mother told you. I know. Your stinkin' sister told us. And Old Clarence sayin', "Why don't you all just stay home if you can only come on nice days?" The stupid shit, let's see him walk down there through the snow."

"You never did anything when you were there except beat up on the little kids. You were still in Grade 1 after three years." Tim felt a fierce rage rise in him. "You were too yellow to touch anyone your own age. And too yellow for the army," he added, just for spite.

He opened the car door and gestured for Marie to jump in, never taking his eyes off Ted. He could see the anger rising in Ted's face. Herb noticed it too and moved back in the clear.

Cursing loudly, Ted raised the battered shotgun high, then brought the butt down on the nearest headlight. The savage blow shattered the glass. It also jarred the shotgun's worn pin mechanism. The sixteen-gauge shell exploded in the barrel. Flame and pellets shot out with a deadly roar only inches from Ted's face. He lost his grip on the barrel. The gun fell to the ground as Ted collapsed to his knees, his well-tanned face now ash white.

Tim strode forward quickly and grabbed the gun by the stock.

Herb ran to Ted's side and shielded him from Tim, placing his arm protectively on Ted's shoulder.

"Why damn, this outfit isn't very safe, Herb," Tim said calmly, extracting the spent cartridge, loosening the locking pin, and separating the stock from the barrel. "That shot almost got him."

He tossed the stock deep into the bushes, then held onto the barrel until he and Marie were inside the car. After backing the car onto the main road, he dropped the gun barrel on the ground, shifted into low gear and headed home to family, a wedding, and at least a dozen raspberry pies.

21

FISHING

The main industry in the village of Plaster Rock, New Brunswick is forestry, and no wonder considering all the forest that surrounds it, but the main interest is hunting and fishing. When all the ice has finally melted from the streams, fishing takes centre stage. The location of favourite ponds, secret lakes, and hidden fishing holes is the gist of many conversations. So it wasn't surprising when young Bill brought it up one day.

He was a pleasant lad who did chores for my landlady. I was relaxing on the front porch when he asked, "Say Tom, ever do any fishing?"

"Well, not much," I answered.

"I know a good place. Only need someone with a car."

"It's been a while, but if you have gear to lend me, fishing rods and stuff," I told him.

Back in grade school we'd fished in a small brook using a hazel rod with twine string fitted with a hook and worms. Bill lent me a slightly more up-to-date rod, and early Saturday morning we headed out.

At the time the Renous Highway was only a dirt track, narrow and rough with the trees crowding in. All traffic had to pass through a gate where a forest ranger checked you through. Once on the Renous, we drove for about an hour, then walked another forty minutes with Bill leading the way.

The janitor from Bill's elementary school had taught Bill everything he knew about fishing, and had taken him to many great fishing spots. This summer his mentor was sick and couldn't fish. The lure of those distant spots was breaking Bill's heart. When I showed up at the boarding house for my first job with a car, it was a godsend for Bill.

The path through the woods was rough, almost nonexistent, and led to an abandoned beaver pond, a rather desolate place, all mud and dead trees. Bill said not to pay any attention to it as he led us upstream to the beaver's new abode. There we found a high wall of fresh mud and new sticks, with a whole lake backed up behind it.

"Take your spinning rod, wade out, and climb up on that beaver house," Bill directed me. "Use lots of worms and cast in all directions. No tree limbs to bother you there."

He departed for some place farther upstream.

When I stood on that beaver house and looked around, a feeling of wonderment came over me, a feeling I often have when deep in the woods. I was almost overcome by the clear water, large trees, and the soft lonely quiet.

My first cast with the borrowed rod brought a sharp splash and a shiny speckled trout. Bill had told me not to worry about the noise, said it didn't matter, had even fitted a heavier sinker for more range. What a ball: it was great. Take off a fish, replace the worm, another cast and another trout. The beaver house allowed casting in a wide circle, so I splashed on one side, then another, with fish everywhere. After a while, though, the action slowed and the biting became more inconsistent. I began to wonder how Bill was doing. As I waded back to shore, I hoped I hadn't frightened all the fish away.

Bill was sitting by a small spring, not far from where he'd left me, cleaning his catch, cutting them open and rinsing them in cold water. He carefully placed each cleaned trout in a pile beside many other well-cleaned trout. The limit in those days was twenty-one trout per person. Bill had close to forty, all the same size: large.

"How'd you make out?" he asked.

Inspecting my motley assortment, he smiled and suggested that I might have put the small ones back in the water. "These four here, I'd have kept those," he said.

I always admire real genius when I find it, and it was certainly evident here. That janitor had discovered an apt pupil in young Bill, who loved the woods and knew how to fish.

When I had waded out to the beaver's house, Bill had quietly settled into the shadows toward the upper end of the pond. Here with the water shallow, and the sun at the right angle, he could actually see the fish, spread out by the hundreds. They were hiding from the awful noise and the loud splashing some damned fool was conveniently making downstream. Bill's casting rod, a gift from his friend and mentor, was his pride and joy. He easily picked off selected trout, never disturbing others only inches away. The line snaked out without a sound, the clear colourless leader placing a fly inches from the fish's nose, usually one toward the outside of the school.

We reported at the gate on the way home. The ranger smiled knowingly at Bill when we displayed our catches, twenty-one fish each. "Those look like Clearwater trout," he commented. "Weren't long at the brook, were you?"

My poor little fish were hidden well out of sight.

Bill gave me another surprise when I let him out at his mother's. Handing me all his fish, he said, "Give all these to your landlady. She's planning on having them for supper."

And they sure tasted good.

22

GROCERIES

When I lived on the farm, I was often sent into town to buy groceries. I would walk up to the counter with my list. My uncle, who owned the store, would bag them up and hand them to me. Two or three dollars' worth would last my mother for a week.

About twenty-five years ago, while carrying groceries in from the car, I noticed I was paying about ten dollars a bag. I thought that was expensive, a lot to pay for a few groceries.

Last week I went to Sobeys to buy a few things for supper. It didn't take me long. Up and down the aisle, and I was soon back to the checkout. They cost me about fifty dollars. $51.39 to be exact.

I took them out and put them in the front seat of the car. They didn't take up much room, so why bother opening the trunk? Remembering that I planned to stop at Canadian Tire, I saw the groceries sitting in the front seat and thought maybe someone might steal them.

So, I shoved them all into the glove compartment, all $51.39 worth.

23

BISCUITS

A young husband was critical of his wife's biscuits. "Someday," he promised her, "I'll show you a real biscuit."

His chance came at a local church supper. The tables were laden with donated home cooked goodies. The husband buttered, tasted, and really beamed over a fluffy white biscuit.

Holding it up to his wife, he said, "This, my dear, is a biscuit."

"Good thing I brought them, then," she told him. "You sure didn't seem to appreciate them at home."

24

MODERN TIMES

Electricity came to Johnville in 1947. We didn't think it was spectacular because we only had a few lights and no appliances. The lights were nice, but we had seen them in town. We read about things of the future, like Dick Tracy's watch in the comics, but never expected to see them.

Then a new movie theatre opened in Florenceville. It showed westerns on weekends. I liked westerns because of all the horses. When I walked home from school, I often dreamed about watching movies at home. In the late forties the idea of a movie at home was pretty far-fetched, like going to the moon.

Last week I sat in my rec room in my soft recliner and watched High Noon starring Gary Cooper. On a fifty-two inch screen, beautiful colour, and clear as can be.

Sixty years ago, I walked along our dirt road and dreamed about watching a full feature movie at home. It's unbelievable the advances in science that have happened in the last sixty years.

I asked my son-in-law Ian this morning about some character in history. He looked at his wristwatch and gave me the answer. It made Dick Tracy's watch look antique. He had a whole encyclopedia on his wrist. I couldn't believe it.

25

WE WERE FOUR

We were four, sitting at a table, waiting for the card play to start.

A lady, sitting across from me, said,
"You were a teacher.
Well I wouldn't want to teach today.
The students are terrible.
They are impolite, lazy, difficult.
You can't lay a hand on them."

"Sounds pretty bad," I said.

A few minutes later she was telling the others,
"When I was eleven years old,
I snooped in the cupboard

and found a bottle of whiskey.
My older sister and I got into that.
Did we ever get drunk!"
"Sure glad I never taught you
fellows!" I said.

26

THE CRIB

Fresh snow covered the lawns and blanketed the small park with the antique cannon in soft white. The street, though, was mired in slush and dark muck from the traffic and pervasive salt. The girl stepped into the slush from a taxi. She placed a small suitcase by the curb and lifted a tiny infant to her shoulder. The hood of her warm parka hung loosely, allowing her long brown hair to catch the wind, revealing her youthful face. She paid for her fare from a small brown envelope. It was awkward, holding the baby, replacing the change and trying to stuff the envelope back into a pocket. She shivered nervously and glanced up and down the street as the taxi drove slowly out of sight. When she was confident that the driver could no longer see her, she waded hastily through the wet snow and crossed the park to the next street. She never noticed the envelope fall into the melting slush.

The new street boasted many large older homes, often rather stately and pretentious with ornate windows and fancy trim. The feeble sun, already sinking in the short winter afternoon, made the bare trees and wet pavement appear somber. The girl held her baby and suitcase tightly and looked carefully around. The lady on the phone had promised a light to direct them. She saw it now, shining dimly, but enough to lift her spirits with new hope. The light guided her to a narrow driveway that led to the entrance of a basement apartment. The door opened at her knock and an older woman beckoned them inside.

"You must be Marie," the lady said, beaming. "And this is your baby. I'm so glad you found us. I'm Clara."

The room was small but clean and neat. There was a tiny kitchen on the right. The other end of the room was larger. It held a soft, well-worn couch, and a child's crib nearly overflowing with stuffed animals. Marie glanced around happily. The place looked so well-hidden, and so warm and comfortable.

Clara was slim and energetic, constantly in motion as she chattered on. "You'll be safe here. Your husband won't be able to find you easily, and if he does there'll be me in the way. You and the child rest up. I'll call you later. You must eat with us tonight."

Farther up the street, two little girls left from school together, warmly dressed in winter boots, hoods, and scarves.

Sarah was in Grade 1. "I was scared," she complained. "I waited so long, and you never came."

Jane was in Grade 3. As they started along the street, she took her sister's hand to reassure her. "I'm sorry. I didn't hurry because we're only going to catechism, and I'm tired of sitting."

"But it's the last class before Christmas," Sarah said, dragging her boots through the wet slush. "We're having a party and treats."

It was Sarah who saw the brown envelope. It looked too new and shiny to belong in a big puddle. It just didn't look right, a thick new envelope lying in the water like that. She stooped down to pick it up.

"What is it?" Jane asked excitedly.

Sarah peered inside the envelope. "It's money," she answered her sister calmly. "Lots of money."

Smiling happily, they continued on to the church, the envelope carefully stuffed inside a school bag. Soon they were with the rest of their class in the parish center, boots, bags, and winter gear heaped in a corner on the floor. The teacher led everyone into the church to see the newly constructed crib, and the tiny wooden manger, where the baby Jesus would be placed on Christmas Eve.

The two girls stared quietly at Mary and Joseph. Jane giggled at the black nosed sheep and the grey donkey. Sarah worried about the empty manger. She nudged her older sister. "Where's the baby?"

"It's not born yet, not until Christmas," Jane whispered.

Marie discovered her loss after freeing herself and her baby of their winter clothes. She searched frantically, digging into every pocket she could find.

All my money, she thought. *It can't be gone. It just can't. Where did I put it? I paid for the taxi, put the envelope back into my pocket, and now it's gone.*

Terrified, she rushed outside, leaving her tiny baby unattended, to retrace her steps through the snow. Finding no sign of the brown envelope, she walked wearily back to the apartment where only moments before she had felt so free. Sitting on the worn couch, holding her baby closely, she tried to be strong, but the loss was too much. She burst into tears, sobbing bitterly. She remembered how buoyant she'd felt upon spying the feeble light, which had led her to Clara, and the warm room, and the crib, and all the stuffed toys, only to be let down cruelly.

Ups and downs had been a recurring theme in Marie's short life. She'd been happy with her husband, Frank, until he turned mean. He seemed jealous of the baby and began to drink and come home late. When Marie protested, Frank struck her. It became a pattern. Pleading never helped. Finally, Marie had been forced to answer Clara's ad.

"I'll never go back to him," she cried bitterly. "He's beaten me for the last time."

—————

Upon returning home, Sarah and Jane slipped quietly down to their bedroom. The lingering silence soon aroused their mother's curiosity. When Mrs. Giles peeked into the bedroom, the two girls smiled up at her, watching for a reaction. Both beds were completely covered with bills, all spread out to dry.

"What's all this?" their mother asked.

"We want to buy you and Daddy a Christmas present," Jane burst out loudly.

"Is this enough money?" Sarah asked doubtfully.

"Oh, I think it might do," Mrs. Giles answered with a smile, before giving each of her girls a hug.

"There's a lot of money here," she told the policeman on the phone later.

"I'm glad you called us," the officer reassured her. "But it's safer not to tell anyone. We don't want you pestered with crank calls. Someone will surely phone here looking for it. If the money isn't claimed in six weeks, then I guess it's all yours."

Marie was still sitting on the couch, the infant squirming on her lap, when Clara came to call her to supper. The change in the girl's appearance was shocking.

"I thought I heard someone crying," Clara said in a kind voice. "What is it dear? Did he treat you that badly?"

"Oh Clara, it's my money. I lost all my money. It's gone and I can't find it." She could not restrain her tears.

"Well now, isn't that just dandy," Clara answered, her voice rigid. "Are you sure you had any with you to begin with?"

Marie tensed at the abrupt change in Clara's tone. Her heart fell, but her determination never faltered. "I won't go back," she said bitterly. "I worked and saved that money."

"Fine, but you can't stay here, not without income. One little suitcase! How do you expect to feed and clothe a baby?" Clara stormed about the small room, agitated at the new situation. "First it's no rent, then I end up feeding you and the kid."

When she saw how pale and tired the girl was, she relented slightly. "You can stay the night. But in the morning you'll need to make arrangements."

A week went by. The schools were closed for the holidays, and the malls filled with shoppers. Jane and Sarah played outdoors in the snow, enjoying their new freedom. The envelope of money lay in a drawer forgotten.

Mrs. Giles remembered it, though. She wondered why nobody called. *They can't need it that badly,* she thought.

With the special day approaching, she worked with other ladies from the community to finish filling the Christmas baskets. She enjoyed the work, and with all the volunteers the job went quickly.

"People have been so generous again this year," Clara, the woman in charge, told her one afternoon. "I just wish that everyone could be so virtuous, instead of trying to take advantage of you."

"What makes you say that?" Mrs. Giles asked, bracing herself for another one of Clara's famous tirades.

"Well, this girl left her husband and she and her kid landed at my door, not a cent to their name, and now she expects me to keep them. They've been there for days now. Says she lost her money."

"Oh?"

"She just sits down there moping," Clara complained. "Well, I can't find her money, supposing she ever had any. The welfare better reimburse me and find them some other place, that's all I can say."

"I suppose so," was all Mrs. Giles said, remembering the policeman's advice not to tell anyone about the money.

For Marie these were terrifying days. She was too frightened to leave and increasingly afraid to stay. She still had formula left for the baby, but very little food for herself.

On the afternoon of the second day Clara had visited Marie in the basement apartment. "I won't let you starve," she said grudgingly. "Not right before the holy day."

She left some bread and milk on the table. Marie's invitation to dine upstairs was not renewed, nor did Clara offer the use of her phone.

On Christmas Eve, as Marie placed her baby in the crib, she made up her mind. She would not accept Clara's callous indifference any longer. She decided to take her baby and leave the tiny apartment in the morning, though for where, she could not say.

When someone knocked on the door, she hesitated. *Frank's found us,* she thought. *He'll kill me!* She opened the door timidly, carefully. No! It was a woman, with two children. Jane and Sarah dashed into the room, each carrying a small box. Their mother followed with a much larger box.

"This is your Christmas, Marie," Mrs. Giles announced cheerily. "Thanks to your neighbours."

Large wet tears filled Marie's eyes at the sight of all the food and presents. When she discovered the familiar brown envelope hidden among the candies, she began to scream in delight. She threw her arms around her pleasantly surprised visitor.

Sarah glimpsed the crib, and the little baby sleeping among the stuffed animals. "Jane! Jane!" she yelled, jumping with joy. "Come and see, the baby is born! It's Christmas, and Baby Jesus is here!"

27

A SHORT WALK

The view from the hotel window was interesting, with all left-turning vehicles cutting through the oncoming traffic like horses in the musical ride.

I was all alone, just me and five million residents of Nanchang in Jiangxi Province, China. The rest of the family was at Walmart shopping. I had shaken my head, but they said it wouldn't be the same as at home.

The street opposite the hotel looked different, a bit older than the area where we usually walked. I left by the front door and made my way through the traffic, dodging cars, trucks, motor scooters, and hundreds of bicycles, along with dozens of other pedestrians, until I entered the street I wanted. The traffic here was light, except for the sidewalk, which was jammed with people. Every little ways a card table was set up and people played a game using cards and what looked like dominoes (mahjong tiles, I learned later). Dozens of others stood around chatting and looking on. Along the sidewalk were small shops, like tiny garages, each doing some particular business. After hours they pulled the doors down and the shops closed for the night. The owners were continually calling to people for business. Young girls grabbed men by the arm and pulled them over to their shop and tried to sell them shirts or jeans.

I was enjoying a game, occasionally glancing at this toothless guy grinning at me, when I felt a tug at my sleeve. A young girl beckoned me into her shop. I went along, thinking she had clothes to sell, even followed her a couple of steps down into her stall. A dozen women were sitting around talking and playing cards. They gave us a quick glance and went about their own business. I could see nothing for sale. The girl grabbed me with both hands, one on each arm, and fairly pleaded with me to enter a back room with her. I looked at the sad face, at those dark eyes, slowly shook my head and went quickly back to the street.

The toothless fellow was still grinning and the mahjong tiles still clicking as I continued my walk around the block.

28

MEMORY

My memory is gone
    I don't know where it went
If I can't find it, then my life is spent
My memory is gone
My mind is spent
Please tell me Lord
Where they went

29

THE BARN

The narrow two-lane highway wound its way northward, sometimes on the river's edge, often further inland as it dodged rocky hills or skirted heavy swamps. Whether called the River Road by the locals, or the Scenic Drive by the tourists, it was the link that tied the numerous small towns together. The road had been a mere foot path when the first McQuaid to settle the river came along the trail in pioneer days. Checking his lot number (drawn from a hat in Fredericton) against a blaze slashed in a tree growing near the path he could hardly believe his good fortune.

He gazed outward from his new homestead toward the long gradual slope leading upward from the village and at the steep drop leading down to the marshy flats that spread out toward the narrow river. Above the road grew an ancient hardwood forest that soon would be cleared into rich fields. His fields. John McQuaid lowered his pack and started swinging his heavy double bit axe.

One hot July day many years later a man carrying a pack left the village and began to climb the same gradual slope, walking with slow deliberate steps. His warm woollen shirt, thick jeans and heavy boots appeared too heavy for the intense heat. He looked older than his thirty years, but his actual age concerned him little. He'd spent the previous night in an empty shed with only a small biscuit for breakfast. The enticing view as he climbed higher did not interest him much either. He vaguely remembered a similar slope somewhere in Normandy, a grain field leading toward a deadly bullet-strewn ridge. The empty, listless years that had followed—of drink, unemployment, and waste—seemed only a fog, a passing shadow.

At the summit, even older memories surfaced—maybe it was the cool breeze blowing from the river, or the scent of new mown hay, or the sight of the well-kept barn and farmhouse and a rich pasture stocked with black and white cows. Memories of youth, hard work, and pleasant meals. The travel-worn man made up his mind. It was a decision he never regretted. He quickened his pace up the dirt lane.

Mrs. Mary McQuaid had just stepped out of the kitchen to call her husband Bob in for lunch when she noticed the stranger approaching their wide veranda.

"Hello," she called pleasantly, taking in the man's worn clothes and small pack. "How can we help you?"

"Hello yourself, ma'am," the man responded, encouraged by the friendly greeting. "Could I fork some hay for a hot meal?"

Bob McQuaid had just crossed from the barn. "Can you heft a bale?" he asked sternly.

The two men looked one another other over. Casually, one might have thought; in reality a deep searching analysis. Each liked what they saw.

"My name's Jack McNair. I'm sure I can heave a bale or two."

Jack and Bob shook hands. The McQuaids gave Jack the hired hand's room on the second floor of the house. Thirty years later, Jack was still living there.

Tim had a teaching job waiting for him in Lakeview when he married. His work at the school went well, the marriage even better. After the birth of their second child the apartment started to feel a little too small. Tim and Marie soon discovered that any house they liked in town was out of reach in price. A farm boy at heart, Tim looked toward the surrounding farmland. About ten miles south, on the River Road, they found a beautiful bungalow, lots of room for a garden, and even a small woodlot. It needed some work but the price was reasonable. Within one month of moving in they were eating their first radish. That evening, sitting on their small porch, they wondered what could be done to improve their new home.

"Someday I'd like a new kitchen," Marie suggested. "With a built-in dishwasher and modern cupboards."

Tim gave his wife a fond smile. "Do

you know what I'd like? On that knoll above the corn, just this side of the big maple, someday I'm going to build a barn."

"What do we need a barn for?" Marie laughed. "We only have one acre of land. I hope my kitchen comes first."

"Of course," Tim said, placing his hand comfortingly over hers. "I'm in no hurry. I'd just like to sit here in the evening and look up at my barn."

The years went by. There were more children. The kitchen was built. There were hockey games, figure skating, piano and swimming lessons. Many gardens were planted, weeded, and harvested.

Other staff members often kidded him. "Tim, did you build the barn yet?"

Then one day it happened. "Tim," another teacher said excitedly. "Mrs. McQuaid, has the farm up on the hill, I hear she wants her barn torn down."

When Tim drove up the dirt lane, he saw the same fields, the same barn and farmhouse that Jack McNair had seen that fateful day years before. The years, though, in their inscrutable way, had created many subtle changes. No Holsteins grazed in a green pasture field by the road, and the sweet scent of new mown hay no longer filled the clear country air. The house begged for a new coat of paint and the veranda needed repair rather badly. But the barn was beautiful. The roof sagged like a spent horse, one shed had collapsed, and the large front doors were all askew, but the weathered barn boards were sun-bleached and grey, everything Tim desired.

He climbed down from his faded pickup and stepped past the twisted doors to check the barn's interior. The huge beams were still sound. The steel roof still kept the rain out. The stables were empty and unused. There was no smell of decay, no odour of fresh manure, just a familiar musty barn smell. Tim liked that smell. He also liked the sight of the big farm wagon on the central barn floor. A quick glance into a storage bay revealed various old-fashioned farm implements. He stepped back out into the bright sunlight.

Mary McQuaid, alert and active for her age, didn't miss much that happened on her hill. She'd seen the truck drive up and the young man inspect the barn. She called to him when he came out. She had lost none of her charm over the years. Soon Tim was seated on the veranda with a cup of hot tea in his hand. The view was magnificent as he looked past the highway, out over the wide wet flats and tall waving grass that spread toward the river.

After pleasant introductions, and in between cookies, Tim came right to the point. "I heard you want the barn taken down."

"I asked Bob to tear the old thing down when he first stopped using it," Mary said. "He wouldn't even discuss it.

His father built that barn. It was like family."

Mary loved to talk, and Tim was a good listener. Mary looked over at the aging building, her mind far away. "It can't be fixed up. I hate to see it that way. Would you take care of it for me? I'll pay you well."

It was soon agreed. Tim wouldn't take any money. Mary said he could keep all the boards, beams, rafters, anything he found, even the big wagon. She'd pay a truck to haul away the debris and a bulldozer to clean up the site.

"Remember," Tim said, as they shook hands. "I'm not very fast. I'm still teaching, and I'll need all summer."

"I've been waiting for years," Mary answered with a smile. "Another won't matter."

On the very next Saturday Tim was at work with a hammer and wrecking bar. He handled each board with care and piled them so as not to scratch the finish. He loaded the pickup in four hours. One hour after that, following tea and a pleasant chat on the veranda, he left for home.

The following Saturday Tim was at the barn early, eager to put in a full day's work. He'd prepared a lunch for noon and planned to put two loads up. Around ten am he noticed that two joggers out for their morning run had stopped to check things out. *Must be time for a break,* he thought. He laid his hammer down and dug out a pop. Sitting on a newly exposed sill, he waited for them to approach.

The taller of the two spoke first. "You're a teacher in Lakeview."

"Are you asking me or telling me?" Tim said, smiling to indicate he was joking.

The women returned his smile, and the ice was effectively broken.

"Why would a teacher waste time tearing down an old barn?" the second jogger asked.

"I just happen to like barns," Tim told

her. "We'll use the beams to build a smaller version down the road at our place. Our barn will have a hip roof, a small red door in front, and even a picture window."

The two joggers exchanged glances.

Tim saw that they didn't believe him. "I found the window at a yard sale," he added. "We've had it for two years now."

"You're not looking for the money?" the first jogger asked.

Tim was intrigued. This explained his two visitors' detour past the old barn. Hardly their normal route, he suspected. "What money?"

"Old Jack," the first jogger said. "The hired hand. He's supposed to have hidden all his money in the barn."

"No one ever saw him spend it, not a bit of it," the second jogger said. "The McQuaids paid Jack real good when the farm was producing, and he had his war pension on top of that."

"Unless he took it all with him," the tall woman laughed.

With this last remark the pair trotted on toward the driveway. When they turned to wave, Tim knew they'd be back.

"I'll let you know when I find it," he called after them.

The rest of June seemed to be tied up, either the garden, or the yard, or even schoolwork. In July, Tim took his family to Fundy Park for two weeks. After that Tim finally got the chance he'd been waiting for, the opportunity to do some real barn work. Tough work and long days soon had all the valuable outside boards down. Then he carefully stripped the metal from the roof. He saved everything that could be used again. The rafters came next. There were no nails in the framework; the beams had been held together with wooden pins and carefully sawed mortises. The fit was so perfect that Tim found it difficult to pry the joints loose even after removing the pins. Some of the tenons had to be sawed, but it didn't matter as the new barn would be smaller.

The joggers became regular visitors, and they often talked about Jack McNair. What had he done with his war pension, his old age security, and his pay? He never set foot in a bank, never bought clothes or spent money on cars, and Mary McQuaid didn't allow drinking or smoking on the property. Jack had hidden it in the barn all right, the joggers assured Tim.

Tim often ate his lunch on the veranda at noon, and Mary McQuaid never failed to invite him back for tea about three. She always had a treat too, sandwiches or cookies. She knew about working men, she claimed, she'd had three of them. Tim soon began to look forward to her stories.

"Bob and I married soon as he got back from the war," she told him one day. "The barn helped us make a good living until the government told us we had to modernize it or stop selling milk. Well,

Bob said it'd never pay, not enough land or fresh milk quota."

Every day the story continued. "We have one son, Hugh, and four dear grandchildren. They visit me every week. Hugh didn't want to farm. He's an engineer today, works at the mill across the river."

One day Jack's name came up.

"Hugh had a summer job the year Jack came. He needed college money. Jack was shell-shocked, you know. Bob saw it right away. He'd seen a lot in the war, though he never talked about it much. Jack never applied for a veteran's pension, said he'd never earned one. Felt the war had destroyed his life. Bob made sure Jack got every cent of it.

"With Hugh gone, Jack was invaluable to us. Right up until we had to sell the Holsteins. That was a sad day. Jack wanted to pay us board. Bob wouldn't hear of it. Bob died a year ago last Easter. His heart gave out, only seventy-six. Jack was killed about six months later, upset the tractor. I always wondered about that accident. He was four years younger than Bob."

"How old are you, Mrs. McQuaid?" Tim asked.

"I'll be seventy-six in September," she replied.

"A young seventy-six, I'd say," Tim told her sincerely.

The stories and rumours finally had an effect on Tim. One day he looked over an ancient thresher stored in the barn. He wondered how much value it might have as an antique. He noticed an obscure compartment tucked below the beaters. *That's it*, he thought, *a perfect hiding place*. But it only held some tools and rare thresher parts.

He took the inside walls down, dismantled mangers, grain bins and feeding chutes, and took the floors up. Along the way he unearthed several potentially excellent hiding places. Maybe the joggers were right. The more he contemplated the possibility the more excited he got. The thought of all that potentially hidden money did possess an undeniable allure. What had Jack done with all his money if he hadn't spent it? Had he hidden it or given it all away? Each new board Tim ripped up could reveal the secret.

One day he found a panel nailed between two uprights. A horizontal crossbeam behind it formed a hidden shelf. Tim carefully pried the panel loose. He counted fifty-two empty rum bottles neatly stashed out of sight, about twenty Palm Breeze and thirty-two Bacardi. Tim's hopes for hidden treasure faded. He remembered the upset tractor and felt sad.

Tim finally finished the job, hauling the huge beams to their new site. He marvelled at the skill required to wield the axe that had hewn them. A bulldozer cleared away the foundation stones and levelled the ground. Tim raked the soil smooth and sowed some grass seed.

"I've waited a long time for this,"

Mrs. McQuaid told him. "I can see the road and the river so much better."

Tim was pleased to be finished too. He complimented Mrs. McQuaid on the gorgeous view. He didn't mention the tangled fence, or the weedy unkempt field that had once pastured the valuable milk cows. It was on both their minds though. They found themselves looking at the house, at its peeling paint and shaky veranda.

"Oh Tim," she asked. "Could you find time to replace some boards on my porch and maybe fit some new posts in?"

Tim had already spent more time on the barn than planned, and work was piling up at home.

"I'll pay you," Mrs. McQuaid added.

"If I can fit it in," Tim told her.

He stopped by on a Friday afternoon, ripped out the rotten boards and measured the posts. He wrote down a list of supplies and warned Mrs. McQuaid not to fall in the hole. She laughed. They talked awhile. *Some chipper*, Tim thought, *for a lady her age.*

"I'll be back to nail these next Wednesday," he told her before leaving.

———

Mrs. McQuaid's son Hugh called that Sunday evening. "I have some bad news," he told Tim. "Mom died last night."

Tim was stunned. She'd seemed so active and alert on Friday.

"We found her at the house when she never showed up at church," Hugh said. "She never missed a Sunday, always drove herself too. Look Tim, she would have liked it if you could have finished that veranda. I'll pay whatever Mom agreed to. She told me what you planned to do."

Tim was hesitant about going back now that Mary McQuaid was gone. He waited over a week and still felt uneasy when he drove up the lane. A small car was parked in front of the house. The veranda was just as he'd left it, a gaping hole where the boards had been. A young couple answered the doorbell when he rang. He felt better immediately. They were Mrs. McQuaid's grandson and his young wife.

"Hello Ann, Ed," Tim said as he shook hands with them. "I'm sorry about your grandmother. She was a great lady. And you two were her favourite couple."

"Thank you, Tim," Ann answered. "Granny talked about you too. We'll miss her."

Soon they were like old friends, their sorrow a bond between them. Tim talked about his plans for the barn. They described with great excitement all their plans for the house. Ed's father was letting them move in as soon as they had the place cleaned up.

"You wouldn't believe the stuff we have to haul away," Ed laughed. "They never threw much away."

"I wish we could renovate the

kitchen, new cupboards, new floor, and a built-in dishwasher," Ann added.

Tim smiled knowingly.

"It'll cost plenty just to paint the outside, and the inside even more," Ed lamented.

"Be sure to have the wiring checked," Tim advised. "A house this old usually needs everything replaced."

"Oh, it's still sound, a well-built farmhouse. It'll be beautiful when we get it fixed up," Ed boasted.

"When we come into some money," Ann teased, smiling at her husband.

"I'd better nail these boards on," Tim said.

It didn't take long to finish the floor. Tim started on the posts afterward. Soon there was only the painting left to do, which would only take Tim a few hours some afternoon before school resumed.

About three pm two days later Tim drove back up the narrow dirt lane. He saw a pickup parked near the end of the house and heard the scraping of sandpaper from the kitchen. He decided to finish the painting without disturbing the McQuaids in their work. As he set up operations on the long veranda, he was startled by a loud thump toward the back. His curiosity aroused, he leaned out over the railing to check. Ed was in the attic. A small window had been removed from the gable end. A bundle of ancient clothing came flying out. A merry yell, then more bundles of rubbish landed with loud thuds on the lawn. Tim reacted with a wide grin, pried the lid from a can, and started to paint. He laughed aloud as bundle followed bundle from the attic. *Ed's really cleaning the place out*, he thought.

As the painting progressed Tim became absorbed in his work. He wanted to be sure he finished so that he wouldn't have to come back. He didn't notice when the thumping stopped and a quiet calm descended. His brush went swish, swish… and then a loud scream startled him. He stiffened in fright.

"Ann, Ann," Ed's voice came from the attic.

Tim heard quick steps approach from the kitchen. Suddenly he was very calm and alert. An outrageous notion began to coalesce in his mind. He peered furtively through the living room window. "Oh no," he swore softly.

Ann stood at the foot of the long wooden stairs staring nervously upward at her young husband. Ed descended slowly, a huge smile on his face. He carried two large brown grocery bags, one under each arm, bundles of green bills practically spilling out over the tops of both bags. When Ed reached the bottom of the stairs, he let the money drop and grabbed Ann in a big hug.

Tim slipped quietly back from the window, a little embarrassed at having secretly witnessed it all.

"Guess I tore the wrong building down," he whispered.

But that was okay. He figured this was Jack's way of returning a favour: a kind couple had taken him in at a time of need and this was his way of repaying the debt. Jack's money would help restore the ancient farmhouse that had provided him shelter and comfort. It didn't hurt that it would help a young family just starting out too.

ACKNOWLEDGMENTS

During the writing and publishing of this book, many folks helped bring my stories to life. I gratefully acknowledge the ever-patient assistance of my wife, Rosaleen, who helped set up files and managed the computer, my son Joe and daughters Susan, Shawna, and Kathy for their dedication to the editing and publication of my stories in book format, my granddaughter Erin for her terrific drawing of the deer on the book's cover, and my grandson Christopher for organizing and running a virtual launch that included friends and family from afar.

I also acknowledge the wise words of the members of WEG, the "Western

Authors' Group," for their helpful critiques.

Last but not least, heartfelt thanks to the small community of Johnville, New Brunswick, for providing the rich landscape and the colourful characters of my youth.

ABOUT THE AUTHOR

Thomas Aquinas Mahoney was born in 1934 and raised on the rural family homestead in Johnville, New Brunswick. The fifth child of ten, he worked alongside his siblings to farm the family's small potato acreage and care for their animals. His education began in a cosy one-room schoolhouse. Grade 12 was a five-mile walk away at the high school in nearby Bath. Teachers College in Fredericton led to a teaching job in Stanley, and then further jobs in Minto, Edmunston, Belleisle, and Plaster Rock.

Always learning, Tom earned a Bachelor of Arts Degree via correspondence from Queens University and the University of New Brunswick.

Tom moved his family of four to Summerside, Prince Edward Island in 1966, where two more children were born, and where he taught mostly math and physics until retiring from Three Oaks Senior High School in 1990.

Over the years, Tom has enjoyed curling, golf, bridge, local music, and immersing himself in a good book, especially historical fiction. He lives in Summerside, Prince Edward Island, with his wife Rosaleen.

ALSO BY DONOVAN STREET PRESS AND BLUEMOUNTAIN ENTERTAINMENT

By Joe Mahoney

- A Time and a Place
- Other Times and Places

By Susan Rodgers

The Drifters Series

- A Song For Josh
- Promises
- No Greater Love
- Riptide
- Whispers Of Home
- And Then There Was Silence
- Let The Music Cry
- If I Could Sing You Home
- After The Rain
- Into The Blue

- A Sacred Peace
- Watch Over Me
- The Light In Me
- When The West Wind Moves
- Listen To The River

The Dallas White Series

- Castles In The Sand
- Like A Song
- When I Needed You

Feature Film Screenplay Book

- Still The Water